Running Interference

Cleveland Clash: Book 1

Elley Arden

CRIMSON ROMANCE

F+W Media, Inc.

Published by
Crimson Romance
an imprint of F+W Media, Inc.
10151 Carver Road, Suite 200
Blue Ash, OH 45242. U.S.A.
www.crimsonromance.com

ISBN 10: 1-4405-8246-7
ISBN 13: 978-1-4405-8246-2
eISBN 10: 1-4405-8245-9
eISBN 13: 978-1-4405-8245-5

Cover art © iStockphoto.com/Bob Ingelhart

To A.C., who loved this game even more than I do.

Acknowledgments

This book and this series started as a bit of a joke during revisions for *Heal My Heart: Book Three of the Kemmons Brothers Baseball Series*. My amazing editor, Tara Gelsomino, loved the secondary character Tanya Martin, and thought an entire series surrounding women football players was not only unique but inspired. So the Cleveland Clash live on, taking their place among sports romances where heroes are normally the professional athletes. (Don't worry. There are hero athletes in this series, too.)

Big time thanks go to Tara, who was as much a part of this series' creation as I was. Her influence is everywhere. Thank you for the email plotting sessions, clip art hunts, and margin notes like "YADDDDDAYEAR!!!" that always made me smile. Your direction is invaluable.

Thanks also go to my husband, who was sitting at a bar with me one Friday night a couple years ago, wondering why I was suddenly so curious about the time he'd spent as the team physician for a women's professional football team. He told me everything he knew about the topic with a smile, and when I needed more, he hooked me up with the people who knew more. He also left me chocolate bars on the kitchen counter when I'd been in my office on deadline long after everyone else had gone to bed. He's the best kind of hero, because he's real.

And finally, to the women who play this amazing game of strength and strategy, thank you. You've inspired me, and I hope my books will inspire other women to not only cheer for women's professional football teams near them, but to also get out and play. Why should men have all the fun?

Chapter One

Mmm. Mmm. Mmm. There was something about a sunny Sunday morning that put extra spring in Tanya Martin's already speedy steps. No dealing with ornery high school students and excuses about forgotten gym clothes. No football practice. Just hours to spend however she liked at her father's boxing gym.

She lifted her face to the unseasonably warm rays and wished late February in Cleveland, Ohio, always looked like this. But the heaping mounds of filthy snow lining the sidewalk reminded her winter wasn't done with them yet. She didn't care. Today was going to be a great day.

A glass door opened up ahead, and a man backed onto the sidewalk. He was so big his body loomed around the stainless steel framing, and his voice boomed when he laughed at someone inside the coffee shop. Her pace slowed as she took in his profile. Black, fitted ski jacket. Dark denim jeans that clung to his tree-trunk thighs. And a pair of designer work boots that had never set foot on a jobsite. *Not from around.* These new businesses brought in all kinds, sellouts who couldn't get through their Sundays without a double shot of something she couldn't even pronounce let alone swallow.

She put her head down and picked up her pace, wanting to pass before she was forced to say hello. She didn't want her South City neighborhood to change, and she didn't want these people getting comfortable. They weren't wanted. They weren't needed. What this place *needed* was people with a sense of loyalty and conviction—people like her parents, who both owned mom-and-pop businesses on this stretch of street. For even longer than her mother had been cooking her "almost famous" pulled-pork and holding twice-monthly Free Soup Fridays at her restaurant, Mama

Mary's, her father had been taking kids off the streets and teaching them life skills with the help of boxing and martial arts at his gym. Those things were so much more important than overpriced warehouse condos and a chain coffee shop.

"Oh crap!"

The rich rumble of words came first, followed by a splash of something hot along her neck, and then an impact that had her careening toward the icy snowdrift. Her hands jutted out to break her fall, but she never hit. Instead, a crushing grip circled her right elbow and a jolt set her upright. Somehow her shoulder remained attached to its socket.

"I'm so sorry," said the deep voice again. "I … "

She looked from the work boots to the face of the trendily dressed, mammoth man, and her jaw dropped. *Cam Simmons.*

"Tanya Martin?" he asked. "Holy shit!"

Stunned into silence, she reached a hand to her neck and wiped at the droplets.

He pulled a napkin bearing the Coffee Bean logo from his pocket. "Are you okay?" He dabbed the napkin at her neck, then her chest. A little too rough. But the swipes that followed were a little too friendly.

She nodded and brushed his hand away.

How long had it been? *Five years.* Not that she'd been counting … lately. Their friendship had cooled on a barrage of texts and calls that tapered off as he got used to life away from Cleveland. Eventually the distance between them proved too great to cross. Who needed old friends when you had a shiny new multi-million-dollar NFL contract?

And that contract looked good on him, too. It had turned him into an entirely different person from the anxious, overachieving high school boy she'd spent hours with at Pop's gym. Taller and bigger, naturally, but there was also a relaxed confidence gleaming in those deep brown eyes. He didn't just want to be good; he knew he was good.

"What happened to your hair?" she blurted.

He'd had curls that rivaled hers in high school.

He palmed his nearly bald head and smiled. Somewhere angels sang. He'd always been too talented and handsome for his own good.

"I like my helmet to have a snug fit," he said. "And I was tired of messing around with skull caps. Does it look bad?"

Sly dog. Always digging for compliments, but he didn't need the ego boost. "Do you really care what I think?" Again, the last five years weighed heavy on her mind. There hadn't been so much as a Facebook like or a forwarded chain email between them. "I mean, come on. You're the Super Bowl MVP. You hardly need approval from me."

"But it would be nice." He flashed that smile again and her heart spontaneously warmed.

Disturbing. She did not want to have feelings for him after all these years. Their one night together senior year had muddied the innocent friendship, and it had taken years for her to find a neutral place, where she could hear his name, see his face, watch his games without feeling some sense of loss and hurt.

"I can't believe you're here," she said.

"I owed my mama the trip. Been promising for years. Got nothing going on until optional team activities in April, so I figured why not."

That was at least a month away. A month of running into him like this.

Shit. She backed up. "Well, it was good seeing you."

"Wait a minute." He grabbed her arm. Softer than the last time. Even through the layers of her hooded sweatshirt and long-sleeved T-shirt, she felt an unsettling tingle. "Where you running off to so fast? I'll buy you a coffee."

She glanced behind him at the gleaming monstrosity that required the leveling of two locally owned businesses to create. "No thanks. I'm not a coffee drinker. Besides, I have some ring time waiting for me."

"That's right! Pop's Gym & Ring." Deep, loud, and somehow flashy, he sounded like he'd already signed his name on a lucrative sports network announcing career. "I'm going to tag along. Say hey. Do you mind?"

She did, but if she made a big deal out of it, then she wouldn't be neutral. "Come on."

They walked the next two blocks with a safe distance between them, talking about the obvious: his Super Bowl win. It seemed safer than delving into their overly personal past. She'd never been so happy to push open the doors to the gym. Her sanctuary. She breathed in the musty smell of hard work and dedication, and exhaled her restlessness over seeing Cam.

"I'll catch ya later," she said, waving a hand at him and eyeing up the hallway that led to the locker rooms. With any luck, he'd be gone by the time she came out, and if he wasn't, maybe she'd throw on some gloves, challenge him to a few rounds, and teach him a couple things. He might be bigger and stronger, but she wasn't above hitting below the belt if need be. Hell, he deserved it.

It was always good to have a backup plan.

She ducked around a support beam and dragged her hand along the red ring ropes as she passed, smiling at a couple guys who were lifting free weights. This was still going to be a good day. Literally running into Cam Simmons was not going to change that.

Her father's office door opened and out stepped a man in a suit. Business on a Sunday? Or maybe church. That made more sense. She smiled at the man and then at her father, but her father didn't smile back. He looked stricken and pale.

"You okay, Pop?" She went to him, now highly suspicious of the well-dressed man. With all the real estate bullying that had gone on in this "up-and-coming neighborhood" over the past year, she couldn't be too careful.

"I'm fine," he said, and then he flashed an uneasy look at the man and made a gesture toward the door. "He was just leaving."

"Who is he?" She directed the question at the suit, who looked down his nose at her.

"Foreman Keller, from Great Lakes Savings and Loan, and you are?"

A banker. She lifted her chin and looked down her nose at him. "Tanya Martin, Pop's daughter." She looked at her father who was shaking his head like he wanted this conversation to end.

"Well, Tanya Martin, you might want to tell your father to pay his bills. It would save all of us time and money."

"Excuse me?" She puffed out her chest. Habit. Two older brothers, four hundred high school students, and a roster spot as a women's professional football linewoman taught her the bigger you looked the more seriously people took you.

"Stop," her father said. "It's not her concern."

"What do you mean it's not my concern?" She set her sights on the suit again. "Why are you here?"

"Just doing my job. And as long as he does his, I won't be back." He pointed at Pop. "You hear me?"

Smug *and* threatening? Not on her watch. She sort of snapped. The heels of her palms hit his lapels and knocked him back a couple feet.

"Stop!" her father said again.

"You're crazy!" The man scrambled for the door, but she followed.

"Get out and don't come back." She raised her hand for emphasis—not to hit him again—but still he flinched.

A pair of strong arms rounded her waist and halted her forward progress. A second later her back hit something hard and unforgiving, and the banker fled through the double doors.

When the arms released her, she spun around and came face-to-face with Cam. Again.

"What the hell do you think you're doing?" she spit out.

Cam's eyebrows rose. "Stopping you from getting arrested for assault."

"*Please.* I just pushed the guy. And you didn't hear how he was talking to my father." She looked around him in time to see the office door close.

What was going on? There was only one way to find out.

She raised a dismissive hand to Cam, warning him to stay away, and stalked back to the office. Her father was sitting at his desk, face in his hands. "Pop?"

He looked up, and his expression crumbled. "I'm sorry."

"For what?"

"Messin' up."

"How?" She fell to her knees and patted his thigh. "Start at the beginning."

When he exhaled, he shuddered, and her already rattled mood plummeted. Whatever it was, it was bad.

"I borrowed money to help someone out. I put the gym up as collateral, and now I'm behind on payments. I have ninety days to pay in full or they're gonna take it."

Fuck. Tanya swallowed against the lump in her throat. How the hell had this happened? She was in the gym whenever she wasn't teaching or playing football, and her brothers Terrell and Tyler were in and out too. None of them had intimate knowledge of the gym's finances, because that was Pop's thing, but somebody should've seen or sensed trouble.

He rubbed the back of her hand. "I failed everyone."

"No!" Those words didn't belong on her father's lips. He was South City's big-hearted hero. "We can fix this. We can talk to everybody in the family, and whatever you owe, we'll pull together and pay it back. It's the least we can do for everything you've done for us. How much do you owe?"

His voice muffled in his throat as he said, "Thirty thousand."

Damn it. She didn't have anywhere near that much. Neither did any of her brothers or sisters. Terrell was unemployed. Tyler's money was tied up in a messy divorce and custody battle. Tori was raising three kids on her own. And Teresa had just gone back to graduate school.

"Who'd you loan the money to?" she asked. "We'll just have to make them pay you back sooner than they expected. Then we can settle the debt."

Pop crossed his arms and hardened his expression. "Nope."

She squeezed her father's hand in an expression of sympathy and strength. "I know you don't want to call in a debt, but no friendship is worth losing the gym. Who is it?"

He looked at her, and his eyes fluttered as they rolled toward the back of his head. "I gave the money to your mother."

Tanya sat back on her heels and let his words sink in. Talk about worst-case scenario.

After a few calming breaths, she asked, "Why would Mom take $30,000 dollars from you? You haven't owed child support payments in years, and it can't be the restaurant. I live right above it, remember? It's freaking packed on weekdays."

Pop sighed. "The Diazes got an offer to sell the building to developers, so they told your mother they wouldn't be renewing her lease. She came to me panicked, and we put together an offer to buy the building ourselves."

What an unbelievable mess with her mother at the heart of it. Tanya bit back a growl. She'd been so proud of that purchase, thinking her mother had done it while standing on her own two feet. A strong, capable, independent woman. When in reality, her father had helped his ex-wife. Of course he had. His sense of obligation didn't quit. Pop Martin swooped in to save the day with no care for the trouble it would cause him.

Tanya didn't want to take sides. She'd thought she was beyond that. But in times like these, it was hard not to. The anger tossed her back seventeen years to the day he moved out of the family home. She'd been eleven, and convinced her mother was to blame.

Damn it. It just proved her theory on love and marriage. Once you loved someone enough to promise them forever, you were tied to them and their freaking problems even after forever fell apart. That's why she stayed far away from relationship strings.

"What's done is done," she said, grasping desperately at words that would help her remain neutral. "We just have to figure out a way to fix it."

There had to be an idea that would let both her parents hold onto their dreams.

She looked around, hoping for inspiration. Photographs lined the office walls, chronicling the accomplishments of the kids that had worked out in this gym. Some of them actually made it onto the few remaining college boxing teams. Her heart squeezed. This gym was so many things to so many people. Her father had even managed to bring low- and no-cost healthcare to the neighborhood in this very space by partnering with her best friend MJ's fiancé, sports medicine guru Tag Howard.

Wait! Maybe that was the answer. "What about Doc?" She jumped to her feet and pointed at the medical equipment in the partitioned corner of the office. "He's pumped a ton of cash into this place to create the training room. I bet he'd lend us more."

"No." Pop's face wrinkled. "I won't borrow any more money I can't pay back." He slapped his hands on his thighs like he'd done her whole life whenever the situation was non-negotiable. "Enough is enough. I've had a lot of time to think about this. And without any savings, my pension alone can't cover all the payments I already have. Borrowing more money would be irresponsible."

"What happened to your savings?"

Pop shrugged. "The house needed a new roof last summer."

The house where her mother lived. Tanya threw up her hands. "Unbelievable." Her father hadn't lived in that house since her parents had separated and he moved into the apartment above the gym. Sure, Tori and her kids had been living there for years, upping the responsibility Pop must've felt, but still…

How about a little independence, people? Take care of your own problems. There was a novel idea.

More deep breaths. More head shakes. "Okay," she said. "There's gotta be a way to stop this." There had to be.

Think, Tanya. Think. Something would come to her, because nobody threw a block like she did. Protection was the name of the game. They'd be prying this gym from her cold, dead hands.

A knock sounded, and she turned in time to see the door she'd forgotten to close completely swing open.

"Cam!" her father said.

"Hey," Cam said.

Great. For five years, he hadn't been anywhere to be found. Today, he was every-damn-where.

• • •

"How can I help?" Cam stepped into the office and closed the door behind him. "I couldn't help but overhear."

Pop stood. "Whatever you heard, forget about it, and get over here and give me a hug, Mr. Cam Damn Simmons." He whistled. "Super Bowl *champeen*."

Cam hugged the little man, letting him slap him soundly on the back. He hated the circumstances he'd walked in on, but it sure felt good to be back. He'd spent so much time here as a teen, Pop had become a surrogate father to him.

"Glad to see you made it home," Pop said.

"Glad to be home."

Cam heard a scoff from someplace behind him. *Tanya.* But when he turned she was leafing through papers on her father's desk, looking uninterested in the conversation.

"Can you give my dad and me some time alone, please?" she asked without looking up.

He nodded. "Yeah. Of course." But as he backed toward the door, he made eye contact with Pop and said again, "I can help … if you let me."

Tanya glared at him. *Woo wee!* Ice cold. And it didn't get warmer until he was back in the gym.

Under the circumstances, he wasn't surprised by her reaction. He wouldn't want his dirty laundry being aired in front of anybody. But he wasn't just anybody—at least he hadn't been. That's why he'd walked in and offered to help. Apparently, five years away changed things. Something else that didn't completely surprise him. He just hadn't thought it would erase ten years of a friendship so close they were damn near family. With one exception—what had happened beneath the bleachers senior year. Thinking about it still made him smile.

They'd always been willing to go the extra mile for each other back then, and after what he'd overheard standing outside Pop's office, he wasn't going to let that change.

When Tanya had time to really talk to him, he'd get her to see he could help.

"Cam Simmons?" A short, chubby guy with moon-shaped sweat marks underneath his man-boobs stood in front of him. "No way! It's me, Goby Klinker, John-John's little brother."

"Holy crap."

They grabbed hands and bumped opposite shoulders.

"It's been forever, man," Goby said.

"I was just thinking the same thing." He looked around the gym. "Is John-John here?"

"Hell no. He's in worse shape than me. Works three jobs now because of the little ones. Hasn't been to the gym in years."

That guy had never made it to a full week of high school classes. How was he holding down three jobs? "Wait. John-John has little ones?"

"Three. Under four." Goby wrapped his hands around his neck.

Damn. "I didn't know that." He'd lost touch with the guys he used to run with too. "What about Joe and Marquis? Are they around?"

"Not around here. Joe's banned 'cause Daria thinks it's a meat market. She don't trust him."

Like Cam's ex-fiancée Sabrina hadn't trusted him. He rolled his eyes. "That sucks." Especially when it was unwarranted. "And Marquis?"

"Workin' in Atlanta. Moved about a year ago. Hear he's doing real good."

Now that was something to smile about. Marquis got out. Hopefully Cam would be saying the same thing about his mother at the end of this trip. Boston was where she belonged. With him.

"Bobby, come here!" Goby waved his hand to attract some guy's attention, and then he shifted back to Cam. "This dude's the biggest football fan. Browns, of course, but we ain't winning a Super Bowl anytime soon." He faced the room and the half-dozen guys who were lifting and practicing footwork. "Listen up, everybody! Super Bowl MVP Cam Simmons is in the house."

Cam smiled as heads turned and eyes widened. Three weeks after earning the title, and he still got a rush from it.

"What's up, gentlemen?" He raised his arms in invitation.

Something about the attention stoked his adrenaline. Always had. Like walking into school Monday morning after a big

Friday-night win. Everybody knew your name. Everybody wanted a piece of you. Powerful stuff. The kind of stuff that helped a man feel important.

He signed a few autographs and told a few "war" stories, but when Pop's office door opened and Tanya stepped out, he was too distracted to do much more than listen to the guys rattle on about football. She said something to her father, who returned to his office, and then she walked over to the punching bags and systematically went down the line pounding the hell out of each one.

"Excuse me," he said. "Gotta take care of something real quick."

He made his way through the small crowd toward Tanya, who was now whaling on a punching bag out of view from most of the gym.

"Hey," he said.

"Oh my God," she mumbled, then shot him a look, but didn't miss a beat with the bag. "You want the bag, you have to wait, Simmons. Super Bowl MVPs don't get special treatment 'round here."

He almost smiled at the exasperation in her voice.

Tanya Mary Martin. Five feet, nine inches of attitude and curves that would get a guy's head bit off if his admiration wasn't discreet. The best female basketball player East High had ever seen. And the most loyal daughter he'd ever seen. This shit with her dad was tearing her up.

"Let me help," he said.

She cut another glance at him, scornful and pitying like he was the biggest moron she'd ever seen. "He won't take your money."

"Why not?"

"Because he's proud." Boom, her fist connected with the canvas. "And we don't need your charity."

"Okay. I respect that. Fine. We'll figure something else out."

She pushed the bag into another and straightened. "*We* won't be doing anything, Cam. This is my family's problem. You are not my family."

"But I'm your friend."

She narrowed her golden eyes. "Are you? Because I thought friends stayed in touch."

Fair enough, but she could've nudged him when his silence had gone on too long. He was a busy man. But now was probably not the time to point that out, so he simply nodded. "I'm sorry about that, and I'd like to fix it. We can move on from here and not lose touch again. Deal?" He held out a hand.

She ignored his peace offering. "I've got a lot to figure out these days, so you're going to have to get in line."

Again, he almost laughed, because it had been awhile since he'd been around a woman who was so clearly not anxious to be around him. "Should I take a number?" She didn't blink at his attempt at humor. "You know, so you can call for me when its my turn?"

"I wouldn't hold my breath, Simmons. It could take a while." She shot him a snotty smile before she turned and headed toward the hallway, then tossed over her shoulder, "Maybe like five years."

He laughed then. She'd always been a spitfire. And he had a feeling she was just getting started. He was going to be taking a lot of potshots from her over the next month.

The funny part? He kind of couldn't wait.

Chapter Two

Sell Your Spare Parts: Plasma, Hair, Breast Milk, and Sperm

Tanya shut her laptop and dropped her head to her desk. That was what she got for Google searching "ways to make $30,000 dollars fast" during her free period. Depressing. Hopefully, the school wasn't tracking her Internet usage. She didn't want to have to explain this.

Sell your body parts. The sick thing was, two days after learning her father was in serious debt, she'd do it if she thought for a minute it would legitimately result in thirty grand.

She opened her laptop again and read on.

Two minutes later, she was shaking her head and thinking, *Hell, no.* Donating plasma sounded like a lot of pain for little gain. Her hair wasn't long enough. Her breasts were dry. And these days, she didn't have easy access to sperm.

She clicked through the other options, looking at the screen through split fingers. Honest to God, it was pretty hopeless when a trip to the casino seemed like your best chance. She needed a money tree, or a treasure map, or …

A knock on her office door made her jump. She slammed the laptop shut and scurried across the room. *Chill out, Martin.* The blinds on her door were closed. It's not like anyone could've seen what she'd been doing. Still, she pushed through embarrassment to open the door and came face-to-face with Cam. It figured.

This was starting to get ridiculous.

"What are you doing here?" she asked.

"Roaming the halls, paying visits to my favorite teachers." He grinned, and it was like a command; she grinned too.

"I wasn't your teacher."

"Depends on how you look at it. You definitely schooled me on the finer points of the layup … among other things."

Yeah, she had. And he seemed to have no idea how much she'd love to kick his ass now. It would be a little retribution for all the times he'd cried on her shoulder after he'd left home only to forget she existed once he got over the emotional bumps.

"Well, I'm kind of in the middle of my workday, so if you would excuse me …" She stepped back to close the door.

He stopped it with his hand. "You don't look busy. Where are your students? Don't gym teachers usually have class in the gym?"

Busted. "It's my free period, but that doesn't mean I'm not busy doing important things."

"Like?"

She lowered her chin and her voice. "You're a pain in the ass, you know that?"

He laughed. "Walk around with me."

"What?"

"Show me the school—what's changed, what's stayed the same. I hear Senora Keeley is still teaching Spanish II. You know you want to give her a blast from the past by showing up and sitting in the back of the room. Remember we used to make up those songs that drove her crazy?" He bobbed his bold brows. "If you give me a beat, I'll even rap."

Nostalgia pulled at her instantly. Life was so much easier back then when all she had to worry about was too much homework or maintaining her free throw percentage.

He was still looking at her expectantly. Damn his charm. As much as she didn't want to make his first visit home in *five years* easy, she couldn't quite say no to that opportunity. Besides, the kids would be bouncing off the walls to meet Super Bowl MVP Cam Simmons.

"Fine," she said. "But I have to be back for fifth period."

As they walked the halls, pointing out familiar sights, the years melted away. Then when they reached the Humanities wing, he raced ahead of her and stopped next to a purple locker.

"I wonder if the combination is the same." The lock looked miniature in his hands.

She laughed as he fumbled. "You can't do that."

"Why not?"

"It belongs to someone else now."

"Nah. Once it's mine, it's always mine."

There was the arrogance she expected from a professional athlete of his caliber. There was something else too, something that stuck in her throat and reminded her of the one and only time he'd had her. But the very next day she'd found him standing right here flirting with the prettiest girl in school, Abigail Glass.

Back then, Tanya's athleticism had made her "one of the guys," and the boys couldn't seem to get enough of girly-girls like Abigail. Oh, she'd heard all about their infatuations. Cam hadn't been the loudest admirer, but he'd never disagreed. And he'd never looked at Tanya the way he'd looked at Abigail. Since Tanya hadn't been interested in being anyone's second choice, she gave up on the pipe dream of anything more than friendship right then and there. She'd told herself it would be better that way. Romantic relationships were doomed. Friendships could last forever. Or at least that's what she'd thought before they hadn't spoken in five years. Now, she didn't know what to think.

A nearby classroom door opened, and a kid with a hall pass smiled at Tanya. "Hey, Miss Martin."

"Afternoon, Brian."

Then Brian saw Cam. "Holy sh ... oot!" He caught himself when he remembered Tanya, and then he looked back at the classroom like he wanted to shout out exactly who he'd just stumbled onto. "Are you ... ? No way."

Cam laughed. "I am. Is that still Mr. Ryan's government class?"

Brian nodded. "Yeah, we're talking about the Civil War."

"Does he still use the wooden pointer on the pull down map?"

The kid clapped his hands together. "Yes!" Then he grabbed his head and gave it a little shake. "This is so cool. Miss Martin, do you know who this is?"

She smiled. "I do." It was hard not to be a little impressed when the kid was so star struck. Brian was one of her at-risk students, and he ran with a tough crowd.

Cam took a few steps toward the classroom and then looked back at her. "Do you think Mr. Ryan would mind if I stuck my head in and said 'hey'?"

"Of course not. Brian, how 'bout you take Mr. Simmons in and introduce him to the class."

"Oh, man! You gotta be kidding me."

There was something amazing about seeing a tough-talking high school sophomore reduced to skipping.

Tanya stood in the doorway as Cam shocked Mr. Ryan and his class. Within five minutes of stepping into the room, Cam was manning the wooden pointer while Mr. Ryan slouched in Cam's old seat in an epic role reversal.

He moved on to answer questions from the class—everything from what his grades had been like when he was at East to what kind of car he drove. When he said "mostly Bs," she rolled her eyes, and when he said, "a tricked out Range," she mouthed, "figures."

She'd never heard so much laughter come from a history class.

When they finally made it back into the hall, her face hurt from smiling, and a little bit of the anger she'd been harboring had released. It had always been easy to have fun with him.

"That was awesome," Cam said. "God, I had no idea how much I missed this place."

Was it anywhere near as much as she'd missed him? Which was something she didn't want to admit. But with him laughing beside her, she couldn't pretend his absence hadn't hurt like hell those first few years. Eventually she'd gotten over it, and now she recognized the dependency for the close call it had been. It was a good lesson, one that taught her to ruthlessly protect her heart from the kinds of emotional strings that strangled people. Her roommate Jillian didn't call her Queen of the One-night Stand for nothing.

"Now where?" he asked.

Considering where her mind had been, she wanted to return to her office without him, but ... "You promised me rapping in Senora's class."

"I did!"

Senora just about swallowed her false teeth when "double trouble" as she'd dubbed them junior year walked into her classroom. The minute the pudgy woman regained her composure, she tipped on her toes and hugged him. So cute.

Just like before in Mr. Ryan's room, the kids' response to seeing Cam was off the charts. They asked him questions in rapid-fire progression, and he answered everyone with enthusiasm—even the ones he'd already answered for Mr. Ryan's class.

By the time they took their old seats in the back of the room to serenade Senora, the students were on their feet.

Tanya raised her hands over her mouth and sputtered a basic beat to hoots and hollers all around.

"Miss Martin! Miss Martin!" The kids chanted.

Cam broke in with the rap they'd made up while they should've been learning Spanish, and Senora started dancing.

They left the classroom laughing.

Somewhere in the back of her head, Tanya heard a little voice spout a warning. *Protect yourself.* In a month, he would be leaving again. This was not something she wanted to get mixed up with. Friendly but guarded was the only way to proceed.

When the bell rang, she smiled at him. "Duty calls. I'll see you around."

"Wait! Can't I come say 'hey' to your class? You know how much I loved gym."

The hallway started filling up, and his admirers swarmed. The way he actually looked as excited to see them as they were to see him made her smile.

What would spending one more class period with him hurt? "I'll be in the North Gym."

She backed away, watching him sign binders and book covers, sweatshirts and sneakers. He was the biggest attraction South City had ever seen. Hell, he was even bigger than that. Nationwide. Cam Simmons was *the man* to football fans.

A light bulb flashed in her head. If she could figure out a way to capitalize on that, she'd have the thirty grand to save her dad's gym.

• • •

A whistle blew and Cam's muscles twitched. *Down, boys. Not for you.*

This wasn't his practice. This was P.E. class with ten kids running something called "the shuttle" and eight more on the bleachers because they'd either forgotten their gym clothes or presented a doctor's excuse. Who bailed on gym? Never him.

Tanya stood on the opposite side of the court with a stopwatch and a clipboard, and the whistle between her lips. His celibacy since the breakup with Sabrina must've been getting to him, because dressed in navy polyester track pants and an East High t-shirt, Tanya was looking mighty hot. Something he'd thought about more than a couple times as they'd crashed classrooms around the school.

The whistle sounded again, and ten tired kids dragged themselves across the white line.

"Nice work," she said. "Now listen up! We didn't have the shuttle when I was in high school. We had the mile. And let me tell you, my mile was faster than Mr. MVP's over there."

A few snickers sounded, but most of the kids looked like they didn't believe her. Cam played to them by making faces and drawing little circles in the air beside his ear.

"Is anyone else curious to see how Mr. Simmons handles the shuttle?" she asked.

Of course, they cheered—even the kids on the bleachers.

He looked down at his loosely laced high-top sneakers. Despite the athletic pants and T-shirt beneath his North Face jacket, he wasn't exactly dressed for speed.

Buck! Buck! The chicken sounds started low, but then her students joined in until Cam had to make a move.

"Only if Miss Martin does it too," he said.

Oohs echoed through the gym, and she looked about ready to pop him. But then she lifted the whistle over her head and handed both it and the clipboard to a redheaded girl sitting on the bottom bleacher.

"You're on," she said.

"What are the rules?" Cam asked.

"We start behind the line. When the whistle blows, it's an all-out sprint. Top of the key and back. Half court and back. Top of the opposite key and back. End of the court and back."

"You have to bend all the way down and touch the white lines or it doesn't count," said the redhead with the clipboard.

"Right," Tanya said. "And the loser has to run it again."

"Wait a minute." He looked at the grinning class. "Is that always the rule, or is that only for me?"

They just laughed.

He hid a snicker. "Fine. Whatever. It doesn't matter, because Miss Martin's going to lose."

She won. He blamed it on his sneakers.

"I should've tied them tighter," he said. Along with, "I want a rematch."

But his vindication would have to wait. She had a sixth period meeting, which meant their fun was done. And he was sorry, because it had been a blast.

"I loved this day," he said as he stood outside her office.

Had he known he was going to love it this much, he would've been here sooner. *Damn.* Maybe he'd messed up more than he thought he had.

"It was good." The smile that spread from her lips to her sparkling eyes said she was tempering her enthusiasm.

Same old Tanya. Different too, but enough was familiar to make him think that if he played it right, they could get back to where they'd been before he'd become distracted by his new life. "So … you think maybe after all this fun you'll be calling me soon?"

"I'll think about it."

He watched her walk away, his smile firmly in place, and then he headed in the opposite direction toward the main exit. At the last minute, he detoured, taking a side door out onto the pavement between the school and the football stadium.

Right there. That was where the magic happened. He couldn't see the whole field, but he could see enough to spark some memories of touchdowns and trick plays, sellout crowds and after parties that would've made his mother's blood curdle.

Getting with a girl for the first time beneath those bleachers over there.

He dragged a palm over his mouth and closed his eyes as the wind picked up. That Friday night senior year, he'd gone to his most trusted female friend with a crazy request—sex. So he could get it over with and quit worrying about what he was missing and if he'd be any good at it. He'd been popular. He'd had opportunity, but he'd also had performance anxiety—on field and off. Confidence came with practice, but he had no desire to practice on someone who would make his lack of experience a big deal.

He and Tanya had been so much alike. Too busy tearing it up on the field or the court to care about relationships. It shouldn't have surprised him when she announced she was a virgin too. But it had. She'd always seemed so much surer than him. Thankfully her inexperience worked to his advantage, because man, oh man, he'd been terrible at it, but she hadn't complained or made fun of him. The next day, she'd acted like nothing happened, which allowed him to act like nothing had happened too. She'd been so good at acting sometimes he thought she must've forgotten. But he couldn't. He thought about it from time to time over the years. How could he not? She'd been his first. That counted for something to him. Maybe it hadn't to her.

"Cam Simmons, I heard you were here."

Vice Principal Rollins held open the side door Cam had escaped through.

Principal Rollins now, he reminded himself. "Yes, sir. I'm here. Caused some trouble in history and Spanish, then did some showing off in P.E."

"Like old times." The man laughed. "How long are you in town?"

Well, technically that depended on how quickly he could get his mother to agree to leave town, but he figured a month at least to get her packed up and situated. "Until end of March."

"Nice. Hope we see you around again. I'm sure we could find you something motivational to do with the students if you get bored."

That actually sounded really good. It would keep him busy while his mother was working and while he waited for Tanya to call.

He smiled when he said, "Sounds like a plan."

Maybe seeing him around here would be the push Tanya needed, and his ticket to making up for the last five years.

•••

"If Rollins isn't here to start this meeting in the next five minutes, I'm leaving," Tanya said. "I have a yoga lesson to prepare for." Because someone had complained her classes were too aggressively minded. No doubt a dodgeball hater.

Health teacher Andie Krieger nodded. "I know. I have reproduction diagrams to grade."

Ha! "I'll trade you." That had to be more fun than yoga.

Rollins walked in. It was still so weird to have her boss be the same man who'd called her out of seventh-period algebra to ask her if she'd been involved in toilet-papering the third-floor restrooms. Of course, she had been. Along with the rest of the seniors on the basketball team.

"Ladies," he said with a nod. "Sorry about that. I got sidetracked by a special visitor."

Cam. It couldn't be a coincidence.

"I heard," Andie said. "How exciting. A Super Bowl MVP. Some students were talking about him in the hall."

"Yes. Cam Simmons is a former student." He looked at Tanya. "Same year as you, right? I caught up with him before he left, and I asked if he'd be interested in doing something at the school while he was home. And … he said 'yes'!"

Oh, for crying out loud! Now Rollins was star struck.

"Maybe he would play in the faculty-student basketball game," Andie said.

Tanya's jaw dropped. She was co-chairing and playing in that event. That's what this meeting was about. Spending more time with Cam was not what she needed. "He's not faculty."

"But he's a former student," Rollins said. "And I think it's a wonderful idea, Andie. Can you imagine the tickets we'll sell?"

Tanya could. And again, it was like a flashing neon sign. This was exactly what she needed to do at the gym—use Cam as bait to bring people in, and then charge them for the privilege.

"I'll call him," she said. "I'll ask him if he'd be interested."

She would also find a way to slip in the bit about her father's gym. After all, he said he would help … and he owed her.

Chapter Three

"All right, ladies, listen up!" Coach Howl raised a hand above his head and motioned for everybody to join him on the blue and yellow logo in the center of the turfed college field they rented during the colder weather.

This would be their first pre-season, minimal-contact practice, and Tanya had the swarm of butterflies in her stomach to prove it.

"In these drills, aggression is not your focus, hence the lack of pads. Technique is the name of this game. It's a time for learning. I know. Some of you are WPFL champions." He smiled as a few women whooped in acknowledgement of last year's winning season. "But some of you have never played before. Be courteous. The time will come for raising hell. Now is not that time. That means nobody gets taken to the ground, and no targeting the head. Play stops with two-hand contact. All possessions start at the 40. No running plays. QBs have four seconds to release. Six points for a T-D. Ladies, welcome to 7-on-7."

More cheers.

Tanya shifted her weight from leg to leg and bounced on the balls of her feet. She was so ready for this. Another season. Another trophy. Cam Simmons wasn't the only football champion in the neighborhood. He was just the only one people talked about.

"Gimme Rooney, Martin, Wren, Bell, Bush, Herman, and Jones on offense. Barnes, Wiesman, Lowell, Jefferson, Kent, Aaronson, and French on D. Martin!" Coach motioned Tanya over. "Take your pass sets like usual. Drop and target the defender. That's it. Got it?"

She nodded. When she lined up in her left guard position beside their center, Jade Wren, every muscle in her body twitched. Excitement was one thing. Jumping offside was another.

Protect this house. Giving quarterback MJ Rooney enough time to read the bubble and get her pass off was the goal.

Jade's snap to MJ sounded like a gun blast in Tanya's ears. It was all she could do to keep herself from leveling the linebacker. So much adrenaline. A couple shoves, a few grunts, a drip of sweat in her eye. The ball whizzed overhead, and a second later Coach's whistle signaled a stoppage in play.

Tanya turned to MJ, who was grinning from ear to ear. Hell yeah. Life wasn't living without football.

"Do it again!" Coach yelled.

He wasn't going to get an argument from her.

Ten minutes later the horn sounded, announcing the switch to specials. Field goal work. Tanya carried the adrenaline from 7-on-7 through the rest of practice, and by the time she stepped out of the shower, she was blissfully exhausted.

"Felt good to be back in action, didn't it?" MJ asked.

"Damn good." Tanya ran a wide-toothed comb through her wet hair.

"We should do something to celebrate." Jillian rubbed a handful of lotion over the arm with the colorful—sometimes disturbing—array of tattoos. Seriously, who marred their body with a huge tattoo of Cinderella strangling Prince Charming? The girl who just yelled, "*Par-tay!*"

From the tattoos and electric blue tipped hair to the staying out all night, Tanya's roommate and the team's most talented wide receiver wore the tag "bad girl" like a badge of honor.

"You partied last night, didn't you?" Tanya asked. God only knew where she'd been over the last forty-eight hours. "You should probably sleep in your own bed."

"What's wrong with having fun?"

"Nothing." As long as it didn't blow up in your face, and sometimes Jillian's part-time job as a band promoter had her walking a fine line.

MJ sat at the end of the bench to zip her knee-high boots. "I can't. I have dinner plans with Tag."

Jillian made a kissy-face sound that for some reason rubbed Tanya the wrong way. "Grow up." She rolled her eyes.

"Why are you so grumpy?" Jillian asked.

"I'm tired." Among other things she hadn't had the time or opportunity to discuss with her best friends yet.

"Is that all?" asked MJ, the damn mind reader.

"Maybe." Tanya ran conditioner through her chin-length curls, and then topped that off with a generous handful of gel. "Maybe not." She glanced around the thinning locker room and decided now was as good a time as any. "My dad's having money problems at the gym. Big problems. Foreclosure-sized problems."

"Shit," Jillian said.

"Exactly."

"How much does he owe?" MJ asked.

"Thirty grand." It even felt like a lot on her tongue.

MJ stood. "I'll talk to Tag."

"No." The wet ends of Tanya's hair slapped her chin as she disagreed. "My dad won't take a loan. Cam already offered that."

"Cam!" Jillian about killed herself jumping over a bench to get closer to Tanya. "You heard from Cam?"

Well, that was one way to tell them. "Yep. He's in town visiting his mom, and he stopped by the gym a couple days ago when all of this was going down."

"Damn. A couple days ago? Girl, why were you sitting on this?" Jillian asked.

"So the elusive NFL superstar appears," MJ said. "Is that good or bad?"

MJ had been her roommate for almost three years before she moved out and Jillian moved in. They knew all about her history with Cam, but they didn't know how hard it had been to hide her bitterness over how easily he'd gone on with his life without her.

"I'm not sure," she confessed.

"See, this is another reason we should go out," Jillian said. "Get her to spill."

"What makes you think there's something to spill?" She slipped gold hoops into her ears.

"Because you always hold back just enough," MJ said.

"I'm not holding anything back." Except the fact that she'd pretty much spent the day with him. It was no big deal. So why wasn't she coming clean? "I just don't know how I feel about it. I mean part of me is definitely still angry at him for forgetting about, you know, the neighborhood." *And me. Especially me.* "But there's another part that is happy to see him. We have a lot of history."

"Well, even if your dad won't take the money, it was nice of Cam to offer the help," MJ said.

Tanya nodded. She hoped he was just as willing to help when she sprung her big idea on him.

Jillian gave her a playful shove. "Maybe this is fate giving you a second chance for that night of really bad sex."

"Shh!" Tanya whipped her head around in search of eavesdroppers. Thank God the coast was clear. She had no desire to announce that she'd lost her virginity to an equally inexperienced Cam Simmons under a set of rusty bleachers. Seemed kind of pathetic now that she was grown up and teaching at that very same school.

"Why are you shushing me? MJ already knows this. Don't you?"

MJ grinned. "I do, but we should compare notes, because she may have held back parts. This way we'll make sure we have the whole story."

"Stop," Tanya said.

Jillian plopped down beside MJ. "She said he couldn't find the hole, and when he did, it only took three seconds. She felt more from the rocky ground than she did from his … "

"I said stop!" Tanya slapped a hand over Jillian's mouth. "He would be so mad if he knew I'd told anyone anything about that night."

He'd trusted her, and she'd been more than willing to help him out when he'd suggested they be each other's first—sort of a practice round. And then she went and did something stupid like think the encounter could be the start of something more.

Jillian pulled Tanya's hand from her mouth. "Oh, who cares? I'm sure he's way better now. After all, he was engaged to a movie star. Sabrina Quick." She puckered up in imitation of Sabrina's trademark Botox-induced facial expression.

"And TMZ said he cheated on her," MJ added with a smirk. "I guess he's a lot better at finding the hole these days."

She was sure he was, she was also pretty sure … "He didn't cheat."

MJ waved a hand in dismissal. "How would you know? You didn't talk to him the entire time he was with her. People change unfortunately."

"Not the fundamentals. He's an honest, decent guy." She was reminded of that today. "And he was raised by women. He wouldn't screw one over like that, especially after his dad abandoned him and his mother."

"Didn't he abandon you?" MJ asked. "Calling you when he was homesick or brokenhearted, and then not calling you for five years sounds like abandonment to me."

True. "I was talking specifically about cheating. He wouldn't cheat."

"Well, I'm not sure the fact that he's capable of abandonment makes him any better."

But maybe the fact that his father set the precedent made it easier. It didn't mean Cam was a bad man. And why in God's name did she feel so compelled to defend him?

She muzzled it.

"I say it's a good thing he's back," Jillian said. "He's hot. He's loaded. Maybe you two can have a little fun."

Tanya didn't need to have any more fun with him. She'd had more fun today at work than she'd had all year. And Rollins' announcement that he'd opened the doors to Cam volunteering at the school while he was home just had her thinking it could happen again.

"I say we get back to talking about the real problem here: the gym," MJ said. "Please, try to get your dad to accept Tag's help. Thirty thousand isn't that much in the grand scheme of things."

Tanya glanced at the rock on MJ's left ring finger. "Spoken like a woman who's about to marry a rich man."

MJ shrugged. "Just think about it, okay?"

"Actually … " She hesitated, because after their conversation she wasn't sure she should bring Cam up again. "I think I have a plan that won't involve anyone handing over a big chunk of money. I'm going to ask Cam to work out at the gym on a regular basis while he's home, and then I'm going to publicize it and charge an inflated membership fee."

"Work out with the Super Bowl MVP? It's genius," Jillian said. "I'll help you promote it. We can set it up on Twitter, Facebook, Instagram, you name it."

MJ stayed quiet a beat too long. "There are probably some legalities and logistics you'll have to consider."

Of course there were. She didn't even have Cam's blessing yet. "Let me call him first, okay? Then we can iron out the details."

Because, come hell or high water, she was going to do whatever was necessary to get him on board with her plan.

God help her.

• • •

Cam helped his mother up the crooked icy steps that led to his aunt's house. This place was in even worse shape than his mother's.

The door flung open before they reached the porch and a woman squealed. "Get your ass in here!"

Aunt Yvonne's hand shot out to grab him when he was within reach. His mother's sister was never short on enthusiasm. Or perfume. He coughed as he wrapped her up in a hug.

"He's here! He's here!" The bouncy voice at his side belonged to his teenaged cousin, Corinne. Cam shook his head. The little fool was dressed in a crop top and booty shorts even though it was only 30 degrees.

"Get back in that house with no shoes and no coat!" Aunt Yvonne let go of him to grab Corinne and drag her inside. "You'd better be hungry." She directed the threat at him.

"When isn't he hungry?" his mother asked.

He laughed and held the screen door for her. It felt good to be here. He hadn't been able to spend much time with them at the Super Bowl. He'd paid for their transportation and rooms and set them up in a stadium suite, but between media obligations and game prep, he'd only been able to share one full meal with them.

"Yo, man." Cam's cousin, Detrick, sat on the couch with a heaping plate of food balanced on his legs. Detrick had been a year behind him at school and they'd always been close. Now they were lucky if they talked once or twice a year. Different cities. Different lives. It seemed rational when Cam wasn't here, but now that he was, it seemed kind of pathetic. This was family, man.

"You couldn't wait?" Cam teased.

"Nah. I don't wait for nobody, not even no Super Bowl champion."

The noise level in the living room rocketed to a roar, and hands reached out to grab him. Cam bent beneath all the head rubs and back pats from his cousin, aunt, and mother.

"Where is he?"

He looked up to see Aunt Renee, wearing an apron and smile, coming in from the kitchen. She pressed a finger into her cheek and said, "You come plant one right here."

"Nay Nay," he said, and lifted his mama's baby sister right off the ground. She hadn't been able to make the trip to Arizona for the Bowl, so it was extra special seeing her now.

Over her shoulder, he could see into the kitchen, where a man he didn't recognize sat at the table. Skinny, hairy, and unsociable. Nay Nay's type.

Cam set her down and gave her a look that was supposed to inquire about the guy.

"You're so strong!" She squeezed his biceps. "Are there rocks in there? Take off this coat. I want a better look."

Nothing like his aunts to embarrass him.

The man from the kitchen wandered into the living room, looking about as warm as Lake Erie.

"Jerry." Aunt Renee hooked the guy's arm. "This is my nephew, Cam."

"Nice to meet you," Cam said.

The guy grunted a hello, and then planted a sloppy kiss on Aunt Renee's lips. "I'll see you later, baby."

Nobody said a word until he left.

"You can do better than that," his mother said.

Go, Ma.

But Aunt Renee gave a sad shrug. "He's fine."

"Fine ain't good enough," Aunt Yvonne said. "You know Charles wouldn't let that man in this house if he were here."

Aunt Yvonne's husband, a traveling bricklayer, ran a tight ship.

"Well, Charles isn't here," Aunt Renee said. "And fine's as good as it gets in this neighborhood."

She looked right at Cam.

Back when he'd been entertaining offers from colleges, Aunt Renee had made the most noise about him going far away and not looking back. "Get out while you can," she'd said. As if he'd only get one shot. God, so many nights he'd lain awake wondering if that was what had happened to most of them—they'd missed their shots—and dreaming of the day when he could take them all with him. Big dreams. Some of them crazy naïve. Both his agent and his accountant warned him about the fleeting nature of a professional athlete's income. Relocating an entire family and being held responsible for their happiness and welfare didn't come cheap. One career-ending injury, and they'd all be screwed.

"Can we eat?" Corinne asked.

"'Course you can," Detrick said. "What's it look like I'm doing?"

Cam made a plate and after chatting in the kitchen joined Detrick on the couch. "How you been, man?"

"Can't complain. Your mom got me a job doing linens for the hospice. Decent pay. Benefits. Nothing flashy but it pays the bills."

Seemed to be the motto around here. That damn guilt pushed against his ribs, making it hard to comfortably swallow his bite of barbecue chicken. He did a lot for his family, but it never seemed to be enough.

"Met somebody," Detrick said.

"Oh yeah?"

Detrick nodded. "At work. She's a little younger than me, but that don't bother her."

Cam reached between his legs and lifted a bottle of beer. "How much younger?"

Detrick rubbed a hand across his mouth as he garbled "ten years."

Cam stopped the bottle inches from his lips, and his jaw dropped. They were twenty-seven. "So she's seventeen?"

"One year over consent."

Jesus. He patted Detrick on the back. "Be careful. You don't need any little Ds running around. That gets expensive, man."

"You speaking from experience?"

Cam nearly choked on his beer. "Hell no." But he saw it every day with his teammates. A few thousand dollars here, a few thousand dollars there, several thousand more to prove and fight paternity. It was why he'd made the decision in college not to sleep with anybody he wasn't prepared to marry, which considering he'd been in back-to-back serious relationships hadn't been hard to live with … until now. Now, he might have to adjust that just a bit.

"Saw Sabrina on the VMAs." Detrick whistled. "Looking damn good. You ever see her anymore?"

"No." And he didn't care to. That was progress. Funny how a year after a break up you could see it for what it was—the best thing that could've happened. If she hadn't broken up with him, he would've spent the rest of his life jumping through hoops for a suspicious woman. He didn't deserve that. He knew what it felt like to be abandoned and cheated, and he'd never step out on another person. It pissed him off she thought he would.

"Cam, after you're done eating could you drive me and some friends to Coffee Bean?" Corrine smiled so hard she had dimples.

"You don't need no Coffee Bean," Aunt Yvonne said. "And you ain't givin' any of your father's hard earned money to those people."

"I have my own money," Corrine said. "Please." She trained her gray eyes on Cam.

He liked Coffee Bean. It reminded him of his go-to Huntington Avenue Starbucks back home in Boston, but he wasn't getting in the middle of this. "Not tonight, Rin," he said. "We've got plenty of time for joy riding while I'm home. Besides … " He smiled extra-wide, "I'd already planned to take you to the mall and spoil you."

Her hug just about strangled him, and her screams rang in his ears long after she'd run upstairs. Probably to post it all over social media.

"Nice diversion tactic," Detrick said.

"Well, it sounds like our mothers are not fans of Coffee Bean. How 'bout you?"

"Nope."

"Coffee not your thing?"

"People coming in and messing with my neighborhood is not my thing."

Seemed to be the general consensus around here. His mother hadn't sounded too thrilled about the development in South City the few times they'd talked about it either. But, man, when you got out and saw how the other half lived, you wanted more and more of that. A little progress wouldn't hurt this neighborhood. More jobs. More things to do. It still wouldn't be enough to make him comfortable with the thought of his mother living here, though. But maybe it would make him feel less guilty about leaving the rest of them here once he convinced her to move to Boston.

"You see anybody since you been back?" Detrick asked.

"Lots actually. I stopped by Pop's gym."

Detrick stretched out his legs. "Did you see Tanya?"

"Yep. I actually spent quite a bit of time with her today over at the school. Got my ass kicked in something called 'the shuttle,' but I think it made her day." He smiled.

"She's looking good lately. Must be all that football she's been playin'."

Football? "Don't you mean basketball?" He'd never forget the day she turned down a scholarship to play college ball on the West Coast. *My family needs me here*, she'd said. And over the years he couldn't stop thinking that maybe she'd botched her one shot to get out too.

"No, shithead," Detrick said. "I meant football. She plays for that WPFL team, the Cleveland Clash. Where the hell would she play basketball? We don't have WNBA in Cleveland."

True. Cam stuck a fork in a Swedish meatball and stuffed it in his mouth. Football, huh? Something else he should've known. Something else she should've told him.

This was stupid. He was done waiting for her to call.

"I'll be right back." He set his plate on the end table and stood.

Out on the porch, he huddled against the wind behind a peeling pillar. There was a good chance she wouldn't answer her phone, so at the last minute, he opted for a text.

> *Football, huh? Great minds.*

He hit send, waited a beat, and then typed.

> *I want to see you again. I want to talk. Really talk. When? And don't give me any of your bullshit.*

He added a very uncharacteristic smiley face emoticon just so she would know he wasn't trying to be a dick.

He switched the phone to his other hand and blew hot air against his palm before he shoved it into his jeans pocket and decided to go back inside. Two steps from the door, his phone rang.

Tanya. He smiled. "You called. I knew you couldn't stay away after the day we had."

She cleared her throat. "Listen, I'm chairing the faculty-student basketball game at school, and Rollins asked me to see if you would want to participate."

"Are you playing?"

"Yes."

"Then count me in."

"You don't even know when it is."

"I know what I need to know. Basketball with you. Sold."

She went quiet. "Okay. There's something else."

The front door opened a crack and his mother's head appeared. "What the Hades are you doing out here?" She saw the phone, and covered her mouth. "Sorry," she whispered. "Hurry up. Nay Nay made a special cake."

"I'll be right there."

"Go," Tanya said. "Tell your mom I said 'hi'."

"But you said there was something else."

"I'll, uh, tell you tomorrow."

He smiled. "You just want an excuse to call me again."

More quiet. "Actually, we should meet. At the gym."

"Okay. When?"

"Tomorrow night. I have practice at Carroll until seven, so I probably won't be there until almost nine."

"You can't squeeze me in before then?"

"You've waited five years, big guy. You can wait twenty-four more hours."

He heard the smile in her voice.

"Are you going to make it worth my while?" he chanced asking. There was a pause, and at first, he wondered if she wouldn't answer. Then her voice, smooth and sultry as hell, came over the line.

"Baby, I never disappoint."

Now, they were talking.

Chapter Four

Tanya had felt off all day. Tired. Anxious. Maybe it had something to do with her plan to exploit Cam. Maybe on some level she knew it was too much to ask. Writing out a check for thirty grand when you had millions was probably a heck of a lot easier than agreeing to spend hours a day in an inner-city gym entertaining any whack-a-doodle who was willing to pay a fee. But this really was her most viable opportunity. Pop couldn't argue with money the gym made from increased memberships.

On that note, Tanya locked her office door in preparation for the cross-town race to football practice.

"Aunt T, you got a minute?"

She turned to see her thirteen-year-old nephew, Jace, running a hand across the bottom of his nose.

"Hey, Bud. You okay?"

He nodded, but suddenly the slow nod turned into a frantic shake. He was crying.

She unlocked the door and motioned him inside. No seventh-grade boy wanted to be seen getting emotional in the hall. And no veteran offensive linewoman wanted to be late for practice. But what could she do? Maybe whatever was bothering him would be an easy fix.

"Sit." She pointed to her desk chair. "What's going on?"

He sniffed a few times before he said, "I heard my mom on the phone last night." When his voice hitched, her heart tensed. This had something to do with the damn divorce.

He ran his hand along the bottom of his nose, and she reached behind her for a tissue from the box on her desk.

"She said as soon as the judge says it's okay, we're moving to Chicago." His inhale shook. "I wondered if my dad said anything about it to you. Like, is it true?"

Her jaw pulsed and her fists clenched. She wanted to punch something. What the hell were those two idiots thinking? Not what was best for their kid—that was for sure.

She exhaled. "Your father hasn't said a word to me about this." But she was definitely going to be saying something to him.

"I don't wanna go."

"I don't want you to go." She ground her teeth.

Between Tyler's two kids and her sister Tori's three, Tanya had five nieces and nephews. Out of all of them, Jace was the one who needed to be watched out for the most. He'd never gained much ground after his premature birth and he was vulnerable to teasing. How was she supposed to keep an eye on him when he was in Chicago? The problem was … "As much as I don't want you to go, though, I'm not your mom or dad. What happens after the divorce is a decision they have to make together." For the rest of their lives, because they were stupid enough to become dependent on each other in the first place.

His head hung, and she lifted it with a finger beneath his chin. "Listen to me. Your mom must have her reasons for wanting to move. And maybe she's just exploring options. We don't know what else was said. You really need to talk to her. You're a good kid and a smart kid, Jace. Be honest with her, and she'll be honest with you. Maybe she'll take your opinion into consideration." Tanya hoped.

He straightened, and a small smile managed to infiltrate his slow nod. "Thanks, Aunt T. You're the best. You always know what to do."

Yeah, but that didn't always mean it worked out. She knew what to do about the gym now—at least she thought she did. But there were no guarantees.

The bottom line was sometimes you just had to explode off the line and absorb the blows. Jace was a Martin. He would learn that. And it would make him stronger, wherever he went.

Right now, he needed to go home and talk to his mom, so she could get to football practice and then talk to Cam.

"How 'bout I give you a ride?" she asked.

After dropping Jace off, she made it to Carroll with ten minutes to spare. Cutting it close, but not late. She was feeling rather invincible when she trotted out onto the field. A good hard practice would clear her head and help her prepare to face …

Cam. Standing next to Coach Howl.

"What the hell?" She stopped, blinked, and tried to think of one good reason for him to be here.

"That looks like Cam," MJ said.

"That is Cam!" Jillian whooped. "Did you tell him to come to practice?"

"No," Tanya said. "I told him to meet me at the gym."

"Maybe he got confused." Jillian ran ahead.

"Confused my ass." That was a pretty ballsy move to show up and start chatting with her coach. What was he up to?

MJ patted her on the shoulder pads. "Maybe he just misses football."

Could that be it? Seriously? If she were in Boston for a month, missing football, she wouldn't just waltz into a Patriots practice and strike up a conversation with the coach. Of course, she wasn't the Super Bowl MVP, and women's football wasn't universal like men's was, but still. She exhaled. What were her options? Confront him. Tell him to leave. Neither was going to help her case when she asked for his help later on.

He saw her approaching, and he smiled. It seemed genuine. Maybe he was just curious about women's football. Maybe he had come to see her.

That last bit rattled her, but she couldn't deny the vibes she'd gotten at the school and then on the phone. When she was friendly with him, he took it and ran, crossing over into something almost flirty. She swallowed. And when she sort of flirted back, he looked happy. A happy man would agree to her plan for the gym.

She smiled back—even gave a little wave. Oh God, she was going to go to hell for this, wasn't she?

"Team, we have a surprise, special guest. I'm sure he needs no introduction, but just in case some of you have been living under a rock the last couple months, let me introduce Super Bowl MVP and New England wideout Cam Simmons."

Hoots and hollers all around.

She did her best to look excited despite the swarm of butterflies battering her gut.

"Are you going to work with the wide receivers?" Jillian asked.

"I came to watch." He looked right at Tanya.

Ha! So he wanted a show. *Let's go!*

But Coach had other ideas. They spent the first seventeen minutes of practice working on basic blocking. There was nothing flashy about blocking drills that most guys had done when they'd been kids playing Pop Warner football. Frustrating! Still, whenever she caught a glimpse of Cam, he looked impressed. Lots of smiles thrown her way. Maybe he was surprised women could hit like this.

Eventually—and with more than a few self-reprimands—she stopped thinking about him being here and focused on getting the most out of practice. When she finally made it to the sidelines for a drink, he was waiting for her.

"Pretty impressive," he said.

"For girls, huh?"

"For anybody. I'm thinking you could put a lot of guys who are bigger than you on their ass without even trying."

She laughed. "Then you better not piss me off."

He got quiet, and then he grinned. "You've put me on my ass before. From what I remember, it's not a bad place to be."

Her face flushed. Flustered, she bent slightly to drop the water bottle into the holder only to miss completely.

Cam bent too, righting her wrong, and then looking up at her when their faces where inches apart. Damn butterflies. Her lips twitched, and the sparkle in his beautiful brown eyes told her he was feeling something similar.

This was not okay. This was not neutral. This was ... playing right into her ultimate plan.

She straightened. "You're still going to be at the gym at nine, right?"

He nodded. "You bet."

"Good. We can talk."

But if they kept acting like this, what were the chances she could keep it at that?

• • •

At the end of practice, Coach Howl snagged Cam. "You're welcome back anytime," he said. "Maybe we can even get you involved. The ladies seemed to get a real kick out of having you here."

He'd enjoyed it too. He'd come out of boredom and curiosity, but the sound of pads popping, whistles blowing, and coaches yelling coupled with the smell of turf and sweat gave him enough of a football fix, he would consider coming back—if it was okay with Tanya.

"I'll definitely think about it, sir. Thanks for the invitation."

Instead of heading out after Coach wandered off, Cam hung around until the field cleared and he was alone except for a couple guys cleaning up orange cones and water bottles. He wasn't exactly waiting for Tanya. He just didn't want to leave the field. It was a sickness, one he hoped they never cured.

A straggling football stood between him and the exit. Walking by it without acknowledging it was unthinkable, so he bent and palmed the pigskin. His massive hand stretched the length of leather. Something satisfying fizzed in his chest when he tucked the ball into the crook of his arm. Like holding a baby. Not that he knew anything about holding babies, but the fierce feelings of pride and protection had to be similar.

He spun. He juked. His feet knew the drill. Lighter than air. Quicker than sound. The end zone called. He did it over and over again until he broke a sweat.

He had no idea how long he'd been at it before a voice called out, "Hey!"

He pivoted and saw Tanya dressed in street clothes with a red scarf wrapped around her head. Big gold hoops dangling from her ears. A football gypsy.

"They shut the lights off at nine," she said with a smirk. "Thought you should know that before you start tripping over those fancy feet in the dark."

He chuckled. "Thanks. I was just … " he glanced at the ball, "getting my fix."

"I get you." She dropped her duffle bag and clapped her hands. "Here."

His grip tightened, but then he tossed the ball her way.

She collected the underhand pass at her knees and smirked again. "You don't have a QB bone in your body, do you?"

"I wasn't trying."

"Whatever you say, superstar." She slapped the ball and took two steps back. "Go long."

He grinned. "How long?"

"As long as you think I can handle."

Was that a trick question? If he underestimated her abilities, he'd never hear the end of it. "I don't know if I'm qualified to make that guess. You know, it's been awhile."

Her eyes sparkled. "I know how long it's been."

Something in her smoky voice told him they weren't talking about football anymore.

"End zone," she said. "All the way, baby."

She was full of it. There was no way she could throw a fifty-yard pass. But she knew that. She was playing him. And when it felt like this, he didn't mind being played.

"How about red zone?" he asked.

"If that's all you can handle." She shrugged, but she was grinning.

Tanya slapped the ball again, and he was off, powering his legs like a piston, pumping his arms like they were wings, inhaling, exhaling, and feeling more alive than he had in weeks. He kept his eyes on the twenty-yard line. *Almost there.* At the last possible second, he broke to the right, lifted his arms and turned his head. The ball hit his hands, and he cradled it to his chest.

When he reached the end zone, there were cheers. Tanya was flanked by two of her teammates: the tattooed, enthusiastic wide receiver, and the cool glass of water QB.

"Not too bad," Tanya yelled.

He jogged toward them. "I was about to say the same thing about you." He pointed at the QB. "Better watch your back or she'll have your job."

Tanya shook her head. "MJ's arm is a million times better. Besides, I'd rather hit people."

No doubt. She was good at knocking people for a loop, and the minute he thought it, she gave him a look that said, "Brace yourself."

"So ... " she glanced at the women on either side of her, "a slight change of plans. We're hungry, so we're heading to Mama Mary's. Would you like to join us?"

Why wasn't he surprised she'd found a way to run interference on what was supposed to be their night to talk?

He smiled at the group of women who appeared to be in on something. "That's cool," he said. Could be fun. Would sure as heck be better than sitting around his mother's empty house waiting for her to get off work.

"T-bird, you want to ride with me?" he asked.

Her mouth opened just a bit, and he wondered if anyone around town still called her by the nickname he'd given her freshman year. He sort of hoped not.

Something flashed in her golden eyes.

He expected a flirty quip like the ones she'd been handing out like candy the last couple days. *Baby, I never disappoint.* So far, that had been his favorite. Funny, he didn't remember her being much of a flirt before. Not that he was complaining. He liked the twist to the way they teased each other. Even though he wasn't exactly sure what it meant.

"Jillian drove, and I'm her GPS," she said.

He nodded. Why argue? Whatever she was up to, she would stop at nothing to execute it. That was classic Tanya, too.

"Then I'll follow you," he said. It was probably better that way. If he had her alone in his car, and they carried on like they had been, he might end up taking some liberties, which could backfire if he was misreading her. Super Bowl MVP with a black eye? He had no idea how he would explain that one away.

Yep, he needed to think about this. He just hoped a thirty-minute drive was long enough to get his head on straight. Because one thing hadn't changed since high school: Tanya Mary Martin was just as damn confusing as she'd always been.

• • •

The entire ride over to practice, Jillian had sworn up and down that Tanya's plan to stroke Cam's ego into submission was fool proof. "You can get a guy to do anything as long as you stroke him hard enough," she'd said. Leave it to Jillian.

Of course, when Tanya had detailed her plan in the locker room, MJ had been less enthusiastic. "This is going to backfire," she'd said, and then suggested they all be together when Tanya sprung her idea to save the gym on Cam. Safety in numbers and all that. Because apparently MJ worried about flirty things going down between Tanya and Cam, and she still wasn't sure Cam could be trusted.

What a mess! But if it saved the gym, then it would be worth it.

She walked into Mama Mary's and glanced behind the bar, happy tonight was her mother's night off. She didn't need that added pressure. Aunt Grace would make enough of a scene.

"Oh, Lordy!"

Speak of the devil.

Aunt Grace scurried over to Cam and smacked a noisy kiss on his lips. "Now I can go around telling everybody I've kissed a professional athlete." She fanned herself.

Tanya laughed. "Is it everything you thought it would be?"

"More!" said the middle-aged woman in a hairnet. "That boy's got lips that don't quit."

For some reason, that made him pucker up and lean a little closer to Tanya. Not enough to be obnoxious, but enough to have the laughter lodging in her throat.

Her gaze locked on his beautiful mouth and heat crawled across her skin. *Man!* MJ might be right. This little plan was going to backfire. Hard.

"Where do you kids want to sit?" Aunt Grace asked.

"The big booth," Tanya said. She needed room to breathe.

Cam slid in first on the left side, so she went to the right. Face-to-face was better than side-to-side, wasn't it? MJ slid into the booth beside Cam, and she told herself to relax. Everything was under control.

Aunt Grace reached across the table to set out cocktail napkins. "What can I get you?"

"Miller Light," Cam said.

Tanya looked at his mouth again, which wasn't completely unreasonable considering he was talking. But then he stopped, and she couldn't seem to.

He really did have great lips. Pale pink. Almost blush. And so soft looking. Were they soft? She couldn't remember. It had been too long.

"Earth to Tanya," Aunt Grace said.

Her eyes locked with Cam's a split-second before she faced her aunt. *Shit.*

"What can I get you to drink, honey?"

"Water." She fidgeted. *Get a freaking grip.*

"Coming right up."

"This place hasn't changed," Cam said. "It's awesome." He twisted in the booth until she was looking at the back of his perfectly shaped head. "'Member how we used come in after school for chili in the winter? We'd sit at the bar right there like big dawgs, drinking root beer out of brown bottles like it was legit."

Jillian laughed.

He twisted back around and settled his eyes on Tanya.

"I remember," she said, sounding a little more nostalgic than she wanted to. Maybe it was time to remind herself how badly it hurt to be abandoned by him. That would be infinitely wiser than letting all the good memories confuse the hell out of her. She had to face it; if he really loved this place, then how could he have stayed away so long?

Anger bubbled beneath her pleasant surface, and she welcomed it.

"I didn't ask you to meet with me tonight so that we can reminisce," she said. Her tone must've been severe, because even

MJ looked surprised. She dialed it back with an extra-wide smile. "Cam, you said you'd help with the gym. I need your help."

He sort of froze for a second, smile intact, but then it was like her words sunk in, and the smile twisted into a half-smirk that seemed to be saying, "Finally everything makes sense."

He laughed. "I knew you were setting me up for something. I should've known it was something like this. I'll have the money wired to you tomorrow."

"No," she said. "That's not what I need."

He straightened, and his eyes narrowed just a smidge. "What do you need, T-bird?"

That name. Hearing it on his lips again had the oddest effect. It sort of rebooted her brain, and she had to take a few seconds to refocus.

"Well, you're famous. I've seen the way people flock to you. I figure people will pay just about anything to spend time with you at the gym. My plan is to charge a one-hundred-fifty-dollar initiation fee to new members, which would get them the opportunity to work out with a Super Bowl MVP—you—while you're home for the off-season. After that, it'll be fifty dollars a month for the next two months, which will fulfill their three-month contract. That means each new member will bring in two hundred dollars over the next ninety days, so we'll only need to sell one-hundred and fifty new memberships. Seems doable, right? As long as you're willing to help."

"Sounds like an awesome plan," Jillian said. "I love this idea."

"It sounds reasonable," MJ said.

But she hadn't taken her eyes off Cam who was staring back at her with an unreadable expression on his face.

"Sounds like you want to exploit me," he said.

Technically, yes. But it was for a good cause.

"And for only one hundred dollars." He raised his brows. "I'm worth way more than that."

"It's not about how much you're worth," MJ said. "It's about how much people in a low-income neighborhood can pay."

"I'm low-income, and I'd pay it," Jillian said. "It's a sweet deal."

Tanya gave her a nudge with her elbow. "You get in free."

"Can the gym even handle one-hundred-fifty extra people working out at one time?" Cam asked. "It seems too small to me. Not enough equipment. Two people in the ring at a time. Three exercise bikes. Some free weights and punching bags. What's everyone else going to do, wait in line?"

So much for her big idea. Tanya frowned.

"Good point," MJ said. "There's probably an occupancy limit for fire code."

"I'll have to ask my dad," Tanya said.

"They won't all be working out at the same time, though," Jillian said.

"They will be if you use me as bait." Cam strummed his fingers on the table top. "People will want to know when I'll be there so they can be there too. That's what you're selling, isn't it?"

Tanya refused to be thwarted. "So we stagger workout times. Maybe sell a.m. and p.m. memberships to keep the numbers down."

"Which means I have to be there all day." Cam shook his head. "It may be my off-season, but I have to work out at some point, too. I can't work out properly with people hanging around wanting to talk and waiting for autographs. Besides, I have family I want to see."

Ugh. Tanya propped her chin on the back of her hand and exhaled. This was a terrible idea.

Silence lingered. She could almost hear the grinding of brain gears. Maybe all together they could come up with something legitimate.

Cam leaned forward and wrapped a hand around her wrist. Time stilled. Her skin heated beneath his, and the warmth spread up her arm until it settled in her chest. *Ooh*, she liked that. He traced the outside curve of her hand with his thumb. And *that*. The calming effect. The reassurance. The little buzz that felt a lot like he was turning her on.

Amazing. Alarming. These feelings shouldn't mix with the anger she still felt.

"Don't you think it would be a heck of a lot easier if you just figured out a way to get him to take the thirty grand from me?"

She pulled her hand away and straightened. "I don't want to talk about this again. He's adamant about not borrowing any more money he can't pay back."

"He won't have to pay it back. It's a gift."

She shook her head, scattering the last bits of pleasure. "How many times do I have to say this? He's too proud to accept a handout. He's the one who fixes things, not the one who needs to be fixed."

Cam rubbed a hand over his mouth in apparent frustration. Maybe he had a right to be. Was it irrational not to push her father to accept such a generous offer? But she wouldn't want to be pushed either. There had to be another way.

Aunt Grace returned with their drinks and took their food orders, but Tanya had lost her appetite. She was too fixated on alternate plans. How could she leverage the restaurant? What about a charity boxing match? Were either of those ideas worth thirty grand?

"Let's do some research on occupancy code," MJ said. "Then we can at least have a benchmark for a membership drive. Whether we blatantly use Cam as bait or not, we can capitalize on the word-of-mouth that's already bringing people into the gym. Might as well make some money while we can."

Tanya nodded. "I'll keep thinking of other options, too." Ones that didn't involve Cam, because he was already too involved in her life. It was time to go back to friendly but guarded.

He lifted his beer and smiled before closing his lips over the rim. She smiled back, and pushed aside the voice in her head that told her taking his thirty grand would be a lot less hassle than this—watching him lick perfectly plump, pale pink lips.

Her hot flashes were back. Only they skipped their usual haunts and zeroed in on the tingly spot between her legs.

Friendly but guarded seemed doomed.

She looked away—anywhere but his lips—and tried to think of how to close Pandora's Box now that she'd opened it. Dwelling on all the reasons she was angry at him didn't seem to work. Keeping her distance didn't work either. Not when he kept popping up everywhere. This was insane, like knowing eating a half gallon of ice cream was bad for you but doing it anyway. She did that sometimes. And then she was so damn sick she swore off ice cream for months.

There was an idea. She ran her finger down the condensation on her water glass. Could she just eat *him* and get it over with?

Chapter Five

And then there were two.

MJ and Jillian said their goodbyes and headed down to the gym to make their sparring time, leaving Cam alone with Tanya.

He pulled on his chin. All that flirting and the random invitation to meet after she'd thrown him some serious shade that first day at the gym? He should've known it wasn't about him except for what he could do for her father. She was upset about what was happening at the gym, but she was making the solution harder than it had to be. All this talk about pride and not taking his money. Was that really to protect her father's ego, or was it to protect hers? He didn't know. But ulterior motive or not, the sparks between them generated real heat.

"You sure I can't get you anything else?" Grace asked as she gathered up his empty plate.

"We're good," Tanya said. "I need to get to the gym, too."

He reached into his pocket, retrieved his AmEx, and held it out for Grace. "I got this."

Tanya swatted at his hand. "Put it away."

"I got this," he repeated, giving her a good, hard stare. Unlike the thirty grand, which was an awful lot of money to most people, refusing his offer to pay a forty-five dollar tab was too much melodrama for him to allow.

"Your money is no good here," Grace said.

Yeah, he was getting that message loud and clear. "Then I'm going to stuff forty-five bills in the tip jar when you aren't looking."

Instead of arguing, Grace chuckled and smacked a kiss on his cheek. "So good to have you back! Now you two get outta here."

True to his word, when she disappeared behind the swinging doors, he jammed a roll of cash into the tip jar on the bar.

"That was more than forty-five dollars," Tanya said.

He shushed her and hurried out of the restaurant before Grace could force him to take it back. Tanya came by her tenacity honestly.

The parking lot was barely lit and mostly empty. The winter wind whipped around him. "Am I still invited to the gym tonight or are you done with me?"

He liked the way her eyes widened at his question. "No, it would probably be good PR if you popped in again."

Right. He looked at his SUV glistening in the moonlight, and then down the block toward the gym. If he suggested they drive, she would probably insult his manhood, so he zipped up his jacket and huddled into the collar as he walked.

"You know, that was sweet," she said.

He glanced at her, and beneath the streetlights her smile seemed to glow. She'd been pretty in high school, but now she was beautiful—the kind of beauty that made a man study and stare. "What was sweet?"

"Leaving that money in the tip jar. Aunt Grace will get a kick out of finding it."

He shoved his hands into his pockets. "So my money is good here after all."

"In certain situations, yes."

"But not when it matters most—to save your dad's gym."

She crossed her arms and wrinkled her face. "Even if I could get him to take the money, thirty grand comes with a lot of strings."

"Then you take the money and give it to your dad. I don't care what you tell him about where you got it, and I don't want a penny back. Where are the strings?"

Her face had a hard edge, but it didn't lose its beauty. "No matter what I tell my dad, *I'll* know where the money came from. That's a string."

"Between you and me?"

She nodded.

He stopped, and when she realized he was no longer beside her, she stopped too.

She looked at him over her shoulder at first, and then she turned completely. "What?"

He stepped closer. "Why is it bad to have strings between us?"

When she didn't answer immediately, he stepped closer again. Just a test. Because now that the reason for her flirting had been revealed, there was no reason for her to humor him … unless she felt the heat too.

She didn't step back or turn around and walk away. Instead, her features softened, and her gaze darted from his eyes to his lips.

His skin tightened on the encouragement. *Kiss her*, said the voice in his head. *Get it over with*. If she kissed him back, he'd have his answer once and for all.

"Strings strangle people!" The words exploded off her lips, and her hands popped him in the chest.

Surprised as he was, he stood strong.

"The money my dad borrowed to help my mom? That's a string, and look what's happening now. It's strangling my dad." Her voice shook. Her eyes darted all around. "My brother Tyler and his soon-to-be ex-wife? They have a kid, and as much as I love that kid, he's a string between his parents. That one sting is strangling two people, Tyler and Marissa."

It was like some warped pep talk. The longer she went the more convinced she sounded.

She threw up her hands. "You know what happens to strangled people? They end up dead." She seemed to catch herself, giving her head a shake, scattering her curls. "Figuratively speaking. My point is, who wants to live that way? Not me!"

Wow. He didn't know what to say. Since her parents' divorce she'd been a little negative toward relationships, but her cynicism had sunk to a whole new warped level. Someone had hurt her.

She'd always been so strong. The idea of her crying over some asshole who hadn't appreciated her stirred his anger.

He reached out and held onto her shoulder. "None of that applies to us. We aren't married." That seemed to sink in a bit—enough for her to look at him. He smiled. "We're just friends. Giving you thirty grand isn't going to strangle either one of us."

But his charm attack didn't have the desired effect. Her face twisted as she made a noise of frustration. "That's not the point."

God, he was so damn confused. "Then what *is* the point?"

She growled. "You can't sweep into town after five years of no contact and do shit like this!"

Shit like what? What was he doing?

She smacked his hand away.

Then it made sense. "So this isn't about your dad's gym. This is about you and me."

She looked stricken. Eyes wide. Nostrils flaring. *Bingo*. Wait a minute. He was the asshole who had hurt her?

"Of course it's about my dad's gym." She stumbled over the unconvincing words. "That's all I care about. And you," she jammed a finger into his chest, leaving behind a sting, "can't solve this with your magic checkbook and Lombardi Trophy."

Maybe he couldn't solve the mind-bending crap that was happening between them, but the foreclosure of the gym? Definitely. "You wanna bet?"

"No! What I want is ... " She hesitated. "What I want is ... " She shoved her fingers into her hair. "What I want is for you to forget I ever asked you to help me. Go home and spend time with your mother. Just leave. Leave! You're good at that."

Yep. He was the asshole. "T ... " He reached for her again, but this time she backed away. "You're mad at me. I get it."

"Do you?"

"I do."

"I don't think so. I think you see me acting like this and you think I'm pissed because you called to cry about missing home, and you called to cry about Abigail cheating on you, and you called to cry about how worried you were that you wouldn't go in the first round of the draft, and then you never called again. And you'd be right, but not completely, because what really pisses me off is that after all of that, you can sweep into town and make me want you again."

Damn. Just damn. He couldn't even breathe. "T …"

"Don't 'T' me."

"Okay." He put up his hands in surrender. "Okay, but do I get a chance to respond to that?"

Her shoulders slumped. "I don't know. I kind of want to take it all back."

God help him, he chuckled. "I don't want you to. I needed to hear it—all of it. Especially that last part. I'm sorry. I was a selfish idiot. And while I don't expect it to happen right away, I hope you can forgive me someday."

She chewed on her bottom lip.

As much as he wanted to keep talking until she said she miraculously forgave him, her struggle broke him. "Come here."

She didn't move except to square her chin, and then she looked at his open arms and made a face. "I don't want any strings. Do you hear me? None."

He heard what she was saying, but he was struggling to understand her as much as she seemed to be struggling to understand herself. Was she trying to define whatever was happening between them?

"No strings," he said. "Got it."

But it was probably too late for that. Looking at her shivering against the cold with a strange determination twinkling in her eyes, Cam knew he hadn't completely cut the strings that came from being with her in the first place all those years ago. No matter how much time passed, she would always be his first. And that had weight. He had no idea what being with her again after all these years would prove, but the pull was so strong.

He went to her and leaned in until he felt her warm breath on his face. "No strings," he said again.

And then he kissed her. A smooth, firm press of his lips. No hands or arms to bind her. A sweep of his tongue to open her mouth. A taste of the heat inside.

Her fingertips grazed his jaw, and he stepped closer, angling his head and deepening the kiss on the leverage from her hand that was now sliding over his cheek.

She gripped his jacket with her other hand and made a throaty noise that echoed in the night. Hell, even if this came with strings the strength of steel cables, he'd take his chances.

When she finally broke free, she looked up at him through glassy eyes. "Whatever happens from here, it's just sex," she said.

"Deal."

•••

Tanya took him by the hand and guided him around back to the fire escape instead of going through the restaurant foyer where they could be seen. The last thing she needed was Aunt Grace getting a load of this.

She climbed the metal stairs first. Her clammy hands gripped the rails while his soft hands caressed her ass. Oddly erotic. She slowed down and let him skim between her legs. This was off the hinge. Completely crazy. And she was going for it. The faster she ate a half gallon of ice cream the more the brain freeze hurt, and that pain would keep her from wanting it long term.

Ooh! But there was no pain now. Just wave after wave of pleasure and so much heat. She could run the length of a football field without breaking a sweat, but these steps and that man made her breathless. So she climbed even slower, but it didn't help. She was light-headed by the time they hit the landing.

At the top, she faced him, pulled him close, and kissed him hard. Her jelly legs ached to be wrapped around him.

She dragged her mouth from his and steadied herself with an inhale. "You sure you're up for this?" After their lackluster encounter senior year, they had a lot to prove.

"Trust me. I'm up. I've been up since the parking lot."

Screw the aftermath. She yanked him by the shirt into the hallway, where she broke free of him long enough to make it to her door and slip the key into the lock. But before she could open it, he slid his hands beneath her shirt, skimming her belly until he cupped her breasts.

Lust lapped at every nerve ending. She dropped her forehead to the door and tried to slow her breathing, hoping to get enough air to her lungs. Her head was soupy, but she needed to think ... at least a little bit. Did she even have condoms? Jillian would. Someplace.

He leaned in, opened his mouth on her neck, and she pressed her backside against him. Just a little grind against the bulge in his pants. He rolled her nipples until they hardened, and she gasped. *Not here.* Sex in the hallway when she had family downstairs was an awful idea.

But her body lagged behind the thought. Too saturated in desire for him. Her backside rolled and rubbed. Her breasts hung heavy. Her head twisted so her mouth could meet his.

Somehow she managed to turn the knob and push the door. The second it opened, something felt off. And there went the yummy feelings Cam had delivered with the palm of his hands. She pushed his arms from under her shirt and shook her head.

"Let me make sure Jillian didn't somehow beat us back from the gym."

Something moved on the sofa.

She stepped closer and looked over the back to find Jace sleeping under a quilt Grandma Martin had made. *Oh, crap.*

Cam saw the child, too. His eyes widened as he exhaled. Disappointment hung on his face. *Tell me about it, buddy.* But this was a big deal.

She stared at her nephew for a few seconds while her breathing regulated, and then she looked at Cam. "I don't know what's going on. As far as I know, he's not supposed to be here."

A quick search of her apartment proved Jillian was indeed still gone and no note or telephone message was left. Waking Jace up was the fastest way to get to the bottom of this.

She sat on the edge of the couch in front of his legs and rubbed his shoulder. "Hey bud, wake up."

His eyelids fluttered.

"There you go," she said. "We need to talk."

Cam was standing at the end of the sofa, and Jace seemed to see him first—probably because the guy was so damn huge.

The kid scrambled into a sitting position. "Hey! Cam Simmons! What are you doing here?"

"My thoughts exactly," Tanya said. "I didn't know we had a sleepover planned."

Jace looked at her, but then he looked away. "We didn't actually."

She nodded. "I didn't think so. What's going on?"

"I wanted to talk." He hung his head. "I know you keep a key on the ledge at the top of the door. You used it the last time I was here. When nobody answered, I let myself in, and then I decided to stay. It's true, Aunt T. My mom's moving to Chicago, and my dad isn't going to stop her. He said I don't have a choice. But I do. I want to live with you."

Ugh. Tanya wrapped an arm around him and held on. He couldn't live here. She knew enough about child custody from being a teacher to know it didn't work that way. But now was not the time to argue with him. "I'm so sorry you're stuck in the middle of this." Damn divorce. Dependent people. Messy feelings. Strings.

He cried into her chest, and she leaned her chin on his head and cried a little too. A tissue box appeared in her peripheral vision. *Cam.* He was holding out a box of tissue and smoothing his free hand over her back.

"I'm sorry," she mouthed. Nothing like opening a delicious carton of ice cream, only to watch it melt. She snatched a couple tissues from the box Cam was holding, and then she offered them to Jace.

"Are you going to make me go home?" He looked up at her, and the sadness on his face widened the crack in her heart.

She shook her head. "No, but I do need to call your mom to let her know you're safe."

"I should go," Cam said.

"No!" Jace looked at Cam and then back at her. "Can't he stay and hang out with us? That would be so cool."

She looked up at Cam. "If you're free, you're welcome to stay. We can have ice cream." She grinned.

He nodded, and when he sat beside Jace on the other end of the couch, she excused herself to make that call.

When her sister-in-law, Marissa, didn't answer, Tanya called her brother, Tyler, and lit into him. Of course, Tyler wanted to come get Jace immediately, but Tanya warned him that might make things worse.

"Give him the night to calm down and get some rest," she said. "Maybe he'll feel better in the morning. And by then, you and Marissa can formulate a plan, because whatever you have right now isn't working."

It was all about the plan.

By the time she returned to the living room, Cam and Jace where sitting side-by-side on the sofa, deep in conversation. So deep it made her stop just inside the hallway.

"There's a lot of cool stuff that comes with being famous," Cam said.

Jace nodded. "I bet you get all the hot chicks."

Cam laughed. "I do okay."

Her gut clenched. He'd always gotten the hot chicks. From the head cheerleader to the movie star. And yeah, she was jealous. Who wouldn't be? When he'd had them, he didn't seem to need her. Good thing she wouldn't have to worry about that this time.

"Have you ever been to Chicago?" Jace asked. The way he stared up at Cam with so much emotion in his eyes had her praying Cam would be careful with this answer.

"I have." Cam said. "I'm usually there once a year. It's a great place."

She exhaled. Hearing about the positives of Chicago from a guy like Cam might make things easier for Jace.

"What's so great about it? It's probably just like any other city."

Cam shook his head. "You mean like here? Nah. Chicago is way better than here. It's a lot bigger, and bigger is always better." He smiled. "They have awesome food, like deep-dish pizza. So good! There's a lot more to do, too. They have a pier that runs out into Lake Michigan with all these rides and games. I'm talking a huge Ferris wheel. You can see for miles. And, Chicago has two professional baseball teams. I mean, how cool is that?"

Alright. She didn't love that he said Chicago was way better than here, but she appreciated what he was trying to do. Besides, two professional baseball teams *was* pretty cool.

"I guess it sounds okay." Jace said.

"I'll tell you something else," Cam continued, but quieter. "I'm only here because I want my mom to move to Boston with me. I've been trying to get her to leave Cleveland since I was drafted, but she's stubborn. If she wasn't here, I wouldn't be here. You know what I mean?"

Tanya winced. It figured he had some ugly ulterior motive for dropping into town like this. *Son of a bitch!* She'd been stupid enough to believe he'd suddenly wised up and missed everybody.

"I wish my mom was moving to Boston," Jace said. "Then at least I could see you again."

Cam patted the kid's back. "I'll tell you what. If you end up in Chicago, I'll make sure you have tickets to the game when New England comes to town, and we will hang out as much as we can."

There was the generous streak that had her reeling since the day they spent at the school. So sweet. A turn-on even. If she weren't so pissed about his reason for being here.

"That sounds awesome," Jace said.

A few beats of silence, and she contemplated rejoining them, telling Cam she could take it from here, but Jace's voice had her halting. "If you had a choice, who would you want to live with, your mom or your dad?"

That was where she had to draw the line. Cam Simmons was no man to be giving advice when it came to fathers. It was time for him to go.

She didn't want any ice cream tonight after all.

Chapter Six

Cam stared at the young boy and tried to wade through his own confusing feelings about moms and dads and where kids fit between them. In his experience, a kid didn't need a dad as much as he needed his mom. That was the biggest lesson life had taught Cam by giving him an absentee father. But Jace had a father in his life, and the boy probably couldn't imagine not having one, so Cam would ease him into it.

"You know, it's hard to see it during times like this, but … "

"Hey!" Tanya buzzed by the sofa on her way to the kitchen. "I'm going to make popcorn, and, I'm sorry, bud, but it's probably best if Cam goes home."

The interruption didn't feel accidental. She'd overheard him, hadn't she? And she didn't trust him to answer the question tactfully. Come on. What did she expect him to say? *I didn't have a dad in my life, and it hasn't hurt me.* Or how about, *fill up the hole with professional achievements, fast cars, big houses, and pretty women.*

Whatever. He stood. But the kid reached up and grabbed his hand. "You said he could stay." Jace directed the comment over the sofa back at Tanya, who was fumbling around the kitchen.

"Yeah, but then I thought about it, and I thought it would be better if it was just you and me." She stood from a crouch at the bottom cupboard and glanced at Cam. She must've seen Jace holding onto him, because she closed her eyes briefly and then said, "Maybe I was wrong. I don't know. I'm just trying to do what's best."

If he had to guess he'd say "best" was whatever resulted in the least amount of strings.

"I can't stay long," he said to the kid.

When Tanya returned to the living room with a bowl full of popcorn, she didn't squeeze onto the couch beside him. She sat cross-legged on the floor and manned the television.

Ten minutes into a re-run of *Cops*, Jace left to use the bathroom.

Cam tapped her on the shoulder. "Hey, just so you know I wasn't going to answer that question in a way that would've trashed your brother."

She nodded, but didn't look at him. "When were you going to tell me you only came home to convince your mother to leave?"

Shit. She'd heard that part, too. Probably not the best context to hear it in either. Tanya was fiercely protective of this neighborhood. "Well, I haven't actually told her yet. I only told Jace because I thought it might make him feel better."

She looked at him and rolled her eyes. Before she could blast him, Jace returned.

Cam had said he wasn't going to stay long, but at 1:00 a.m., he was still there. Jace was curled up on the couch with his feet on Cam's lap, and Tanya was stretched out on the floor. The last half of *X-Men* flickered in the darkened room, and Cam had to fight off sleep. Now, he should definitely go. From the snoring sounds beside him, Jace wouldn't even know. But, he couldn't bring himself to get up and walk out without clearing the air between him and Tanya. Not after her earlier admission. He'd hurt her once. He wouldn't hurt her again.

He lifted the boy's feet, set them gently behind him, and slid off the couch. The minute he landed beside Tanya, her eyes opened.

"Can I ask you something?" she whispered.

He rolled onto his side and faced her. "Anything."

"Why do you hate it here so much?"

"It's not that I hate it here, it's just … "

"That it's better in Boston."

Sounded reasonable. He nodded.

"That's the easy answer. You've been trying to get out of Cleveland since the day we met. I used to think it had something to do with your father."

He tensed.

"'Cause you know if it did, it would make sense. The idea that Cleveland wasn't good enough for him to stick around, so it wasn't good enough for you either."

Hardly. "Cleveland didn't draft me. That's all there is to it."

She stared at him long enough to make him doubt his own words. Cleveland hadn't needed a wide receiver in the first round. If they had, he would've been praying they passed on him. Why? *Because they sucked, man.* Nobody wanted to play for a losing team.

But maybe there was more to it.

"All there is to it, huh? So are you moving your mom to Boston because your grown ass really needs her there, or because then you wouldn't have to feel guilty about never coming back here?" She blasted him with those eyes.

"T, what do you want from me? I thought it was no strings. If that's it, then me leaving town and being scarce seems to be honoring your request."

She blinked, rolled onto her back and stared at the ceiling.

He lay there, listening to her breathing, and when she didn't say anything, he slid a hand over her belly and watched the muscles in her long neck tense. "Just because I move my mother to Boston doesn't mean we have to lose touch again. It won't happen. I promise you."

Her exhale echoed in the quiet, and then her hand rested on top of his. She looked at him. "I feel absolutely crazy for wanting this." Her other hand landed on his thigh and climbed until her fingers brushed his fly.

Crazy was the operative word. Messing around like this with a kid on the couch and all this chaos between them. But the chemistry was even crazier than that, and he didn't want to resist.

When he propped up on his elbow to move in for a kiss, a ruckus sounded at the opposite end of the room. He bolted into a sitting position just in time to see Jillian flip on the lights and say, "What the f … "

"Shh!" Tanya jumped up, but it was too late.

Jace sat up too.

Jillian's eyes widened. "Why didn't you tell me you were having movie night? I would've come straight home after the gym. Looks *cozy*."

Tanya shook her head. "It wasn't planned."

"I'm spending the night," Jace said.

"And I'm leaving." Cam held out a fist for a bump from Jace before he grabbed his coat off the back of a kitchen chair. "Thanks for letting me hang with you guys."

Jillian bobbed her brows as he passed. "Are you coming to practice tomorrow night?"

He glanced at Tanya. "I don't know. You might need a break from me." Hell, after she had a chance to sleep on all of this she might want to rescind their deal.

She turned away, fiddling with the remote for the DVD player. "It's up to you."

He'd think about it. He'd think about *all* of it. Now that he knew how much he'd hurt her, he wouldn't hurt her again. So, he was going let her call the shots from now on.

• • •

"I walked in on what exactly?" Jillian asked after Jace had fallen back asleep.

Tanya crossed her arms atop the kitchen table and laid her head in the crook of her arm. "*X-Men*."

"You know what I was talking about, smart ass. How did you and Cam end up here instead of at the gym like you originally planned?"

She propped her chin on the back of her hand. "I was going to have sex with him."

Jillian whooped, but cut off the shrill sound with a slap of her hand. They both looked at the couch for movement. Nothing. How could anybody sleep through that?

"Girl, *I* knew you were going to hit that, but MJ is going to freak. She doesn't trust him. She says he's just going to leave you hurt again."

"She's partially right. He is going leave, and he's probably not going to call or text after a certain point. But, I'm not going to be hurt by it, because I'm going to expect it. I'm going to take what I want while he's here, and I'm going to quit worrying about the past or the future. Just deal with the now, which means fix the mess at the gym." She blew out a breath. "Was it busy down there?"

"Packed. We watched some guy sell the shirt off his back because Cam had signed it. Seriously. He whipped it off, took a hundo from another guy and went back to lifting—shirtless. I was so not complaining. Remind me to have Cam sign some shirts."

Tanya tapped the table as her mental wheels turned. "You're onto something. What if we had T-shirts printed up that said something funny like 'I kicked Super Bowl MVP Cam Simmon's ass,' on the front, and then 'at Pop's Gym & Ring' with the address and phone number on the back? We could have Cam sign a select number of those."

"I love it! I get screen printing done for the rock bands I promote, so I have some connections. We can get them made on the cheap."

Tanya jumped out of her chair and paced the kitchen. "That guy paid $100 for a sweaty old T-shirt with Cam's signature. Surely people would pay at least $100 for clean ones. If we sell 100, that's ten grand—a third of the way there."

"I'll make some calls first thing in the morning, and get you prices by lunch."

"And I'll call Cam to make sure his right hand is ready."

Jillian bobbed her brows and grinned. "Nothing wrong with a little mutual masturbation."

Tanya snorted. "That's not what I meant."

"But now you'll be dreaming about it all night, and ripping his clothes off the next time you're together. It's mental foreplay. You can thank me later."

She didn't need the encouragement. Now that she'd decided to have no-strings-attached sex with Cam, it was going to be all she thought about…until they did it.

Talk about expectations.

• • •

The next morning, Cam perked a pot of coffee, made his mother's favorite ham and cheese omelet, and waited for her to wake. If last night had taught him anything it was the power of being honest, of saying what you wanted. And he wanted her to move to Boston.

He exhaled. Of course, she would probably ask "why," and she would never take his offer seriously if his answer was flimsy. Tanya had asked if it was because he needed her there. He did … but when he thought about how he'd only flown her in to see a few games and spent just that one extended weekend with her at the beach each off-season, it didn't seem to back up the claim. If he needed her, then why hadn't he spent more time with her over the years?

What was the real reason it was so important to get her to leave?

He looked around the beat-up kitchen. He just wanted her to have a better life. Truth.

"Baby?" She stood in the doorway, cinching a worn terrycloth robe with a belt that didn't even match. "I thought I smelled eggs." She smiled. "What are you up to?"

"You've been working so much I thought it would be nice."

She kissed him on the cheek and accepted the hot cup of coffee he offered. "You're so sweet." She yawned the words.

He didn't understand why she worked so much. Heck, he didn't understand why she worked at all. He had enough for both of them.

"What time did you get off?" he asked. She hadn't been home when he'd rolled in around 1:15. He must've hit the pillow hard, because he'd never heard her come in.

"Two. Not so bad."

Bad enough to make him want to jump right in with, "I'm moving you to Boston." But instead, he set a plate on the table and pulled out her chair. *Pace yourself.* "I'm going to pamper you on your day off, shopping, the spa, get your hair done, and then you can get into bed early. How's that sound?"

The wall phone rang. *Wall phone.* He shook his head as she got up to answer it. This whole house was like stepping back in time. Another reason she would be better off in Boston, where he would buy her a new construction with all the bells and whistles, and not a wall phone in sight.

She held the receiver between her chin and her shoulder while she stirred cream into her coffee. "Uh huh … Oh." Concern of some kind worried her brow as she listened to whomever was on the telephone. Probably one of her sisters.

That mug she was holding. He kind of zoned out while he was staring at it. A Dollar Store purchase he'd made as part of her Christmas present back when he'd been in high school. *Mom Rules.* Because that's what she'd always said. Only now one hump of the lowercase "m" and the entire "s" had worn away. *Mon Rule* It made him sad.

"I'll be there," she said, and then she returned the phone to the wall and faced him. "Baby. I'm so sorry. I have to take a rain check on the pampering. Next week. Okay?"

"Why next week? Who was that?"

"Work. I have to go in."

He looked at the owl clock above the sink. "Are you kidding me? When?"

"Ten."

"It's eight! This is ridiculous. How much sleep did you even get last night? You look exhausted."

"I'm fine."

"You've slept like eight hours in two days, and you haven't had a day off in over a week. Call them back and tell them to find someone else."

She tilted her head and sighed. "The hospice is short-staffed with nurses. There isn't anyone else."

He growled. "Their being shorthanded isn't your problem. You don't have any problems. You have me." He placed his hands on her shoulders and shook her gently. "I have money—lots of it. I have connections, too. I can get you a better job. You need to come to Boston with me. Let me take care of you."

Her eyes glistened, and a slow but sad smile spread across her face. "You're a good boy, Cameron. Always have been. But it's never been my goal to have you—or any man—take care of me." She patted his cheek. "Now, I have to take a shower and get ready for work."

For a minute, he stood there stunned. How could she look so miserable but refuse his offer to help?

"Hey!" He followed her. "It's not like I'd be taking care of you forever." Although he would if she'd let him. "Just let me help you get on your feet someplace where you'll be happier."

She stopped at the top of the stairs and looked down at him. One hand on the railing, the other on her hip, he felt infinitely smaller than her and like a kid again. "I'm happy here. My job matters." She glanced at the crooked pictures climbing the wall beside her. "My family and friends matter. Three-hundred-plus days a year I'm happy here. You just aren't around to see it."

The zing hurt, but he had a feeling she wasn't saying the whole truth. Whether he was here or not, she still spent too many hours as a hospice nurse, and when she wasn't at work, she was in a house she refused to update in a neighborhood that was rundown, dealing with her sisters' dramas.

"It's just so damn depressing!" he yelled. "Why would anybody want to live like this?"

She sort of swayed like the words packed a punch, and he hung his head in shame. "I'm sorry," he said. Frustrated or not, he shouldn't have raised his voice.

When he looked up again, she was gone.

Nice going, idiot. He started up the stairs after her, but then decided to give her space. On his way down, he stopped to straighten his baby picture. He shook his head at the goofy jumper he'd been wearing. Fluffy rabbits on mint green fabric. If he ever had a son, he'd never dress him like that. If he ever had a son …

His vision blurred. Twice he'd thought he was pretty damn close. Twice he'd been burned. At twenty-seven, he still had plenty of time for marriage and family. But if he didn't get a better handle on what made women tick, he'd be doomed.

Another photo caught his eye. His dad. The nickname didn't even resonate with the young, surly face in the picture, but that was who Cam had been told the man was. Maybe it was a lie. He'd never met or heard from the man who'd left town shortly after Cam's mother announced her pregnancy. Why was this stupid picture still here?

His chest tightened. All these years, he'd figured his celebrity would've dragged the man out of hiding … but nothing. Maybe he was dead like Nay Nay suspected. *It's just so damn depressing.* He wanted to yell it again, but he knew better.

After his mother left for work without another word to him, he wandered around the house making a list of all the things that needed to be updated, repaired, and replaced. If she wasn't ready to move, then she was going to stop living like this.

His phone buzzed in his front pocket, and he smiled when he saw the name. Tanya before noon? That would help right his day. Unless she was calling to tell him last night had been a mistake.

"Hey," he said.

"Hey. I have another proposition for you."

He grinned. "Clothes or no clothes?"

"Actually, T-shirts. Jillian has a friend who owns a T-shirt printing business, and he's going to make shirts we can sell at the gym to raise money."

Not exactly what he'd had in mind. "And you need me for this how?"

"I need you to sign one hundred of the T-shirts, so we can charge more for those. Please."

First the membership drive. Now T-shirts. "Are you ever going to call me about something not related to the gym?"

"Like what?" she asked slow and low and awfully sexy.

"You know what."

She chuckled. "I don't know. You'll have to wait and see. The gym is my first priority. Sign those shirts for me, and you might be surprised at how much I call."

Oh, yeah? How soon could he sign 'em?

"Great!" Tanya slammed her locker extra hard. "Every idea I have hits a wall." A week into this mess, and she should've had a feasible plan in place for more than sleeping with Cam. She growled and hit her locker again. "I need to talk to my dad."

Forty-five minutes later, she walked into the gym with Jillian and MJ behind her.

"Damn. It's dead in here." Jillian said. "I thought word about Cam was supposed to be packing them in."

"It's late," MJ said. "Maybe it was busier a few hours ago."

"Yeah, well, to raise thirty grand, we don't have an hour to spare."

She pulled out her phone and typed a text to Cam: *If you aren't too busy, maybe you could stop by the gym. I'm here.*

Out of the corner of her eye, she saw her father shuffle into his office. "I'll be right back."

She found him hunched over his desk. A calculator sat to the right of a pile of papers. Bills. She frowned. He'd spent his whole life making life better for other people. Now, she had to make life better for him.

"Pop?"

He looked up and smiled, but it was weak and faded in a flash. "How's my girl?"

"Worried."

He waved off her worry. "How was practice?"

She perched on a stack of boxes near the door. "Don't change the subject. We're going to talk about the gym first, and then I'll tell you about practice."

He nodded.

"Nobody's out there. Was it busier earlier?"

"It's been slow all the way around."

Damn it! "We've got to do something to bring more people into the gym, and we've got to do something to put more cash in the account. My ideas aren't panning out, but I'm going to keep trying. If I can't come up with anything workable, you're going to have to take the money from Tag or Cam. Both men have offered multiple times, and both men have money to give." He opened his mouth to protest, and she silenced him with a raised hand. "I know you don't like that. I don't like it either—for lots of reasons—but I don't like the idea of you losing the gym more."

"There's a buyer," he said.

She lost her balance and almost spilled to the floor, catching herself on the doorjamb. "What?"

"The same people who wanted to buy your mother's building came in today. Me and Terrell met with them, and they offered to pay enough to settle the debt and leave me with extra."

"No!" She was hit with a twinge of jealousy wrapped in worry over the fact that it had been Terrell at the meeting instead of her. Back in middle school, when her parents had split, it hadn't been her brothers stepping up with every excuse under the sun to keep the family intact. It had been her. She was the protector. And job or no job, she should've been here when Pop met with the investors. "You said 'no' right?"

He just looked at her.

"Pop!"

"I said I'd think about it. I got less than ninety days, Tanya. What are the chances I'm gonna raise thirty grand on my own? Selling gets me out of debt."

"It also gets you out of gym ownership." She shook her head. This couldn't be happening. He couldn't be seriously considering it. And if he was, it was only because she hadn't done enough to fix it. "You've got to give me a little more time. *Please.*" She folded her hands in prayer. "I'll have an honest-to-God money making plan to you by the end of the day tomorrow. Do not sell. You hear me? Do not sell."

"Tomorrow, Tanya. That's the best I can do. I don't want these guys to think I'm not serious." His fingers shook as he lifted a key off his desk and held it out to her. "Could you lock up? I need to get out of here."

The stress was going to kill him.

Fifteen minutes later she'd burned off some of the debilitating fear and frustration with a dead-sprint on the exercise bike.

"Candy bar sale," Jillian said from the bike beside her. "Kids do it all the time."

"And make thirty grand?" Tanya shook her head. "What about a 50/50?"

"We'd have to sell sixty grand to make thirty," MJ said from the bike on Tanya's other side. "That would probably take too long. We need to think bolder."

"Maybe we can get a car donated and sell chances," Jillian said.

MJ nodded. "Tag's hospital raises a lot of money every year by having an auction that includes cars and exotic trips and jewelry. It's huge. But you have to know people who are willing to donate those things."

Tanya didn't know anybody with merchandise like that. Where was she going to get items with high-dollar value for free?

Cam walked in, smile on his face. He had no idea what he was walking into.

"What's he doing here?" MJ asked.

Tanya cringed. "I asked him to come when I thought selling gym memberships was my only problem."

She dialed back the resistance on the bike and settled on a slower pace for cool down. He made his way to her, looking mighty fine in sweatpants, running shoes, and his fitted ski jacket. He stopped off to talk to the few guys who were lifting weights, which gave her more time to admire him. The way he towered over the normal-sized men. The way his smile lit up the room. The way each flash of his eyes in her direction told her he was completely aware of her.

Her pulse jumped and her heart raced. So much for cooling down. But, hey, for a few blissful seconds the gym dilemma wasn't the top thought on her mind.

"Ladies," he said, when he was within earshot. He wiggled his hand in the air like he was signing something. "I got my right hand ready."

Jillian burst out laughing.

If Tanya could've kicked her while maintaining her speed and dignity, she would have. That woman needed a sock in her mouth.

"What's so funny?" MJ asked.

Tanya cleared her throat. "Nothing." She focused on Cam. "Actually, Pop just told me he got an offer to sell the gym, and he looks like he's really considering it."

"No!" Cam said.

"Yes."

"Where are those T-shirts? Let me get to signing."

"We need something bigger."

"Something bigger than me?"

God, her brain went totally gutter in the middle of the gym crisis. Why did she even assume he was big down there just because he was big everywhere else? She started pedaling faster.

"Foot-long sub sales?" Jillian offered, giggling.

This time Tanya turned her head and gave her a death stare.

Then she looked at Cam. "You want to throw a few punches? I need to blow off some steam."

• • •

It had been a lot of years since Cam had been in the ring with Tanya. He was bigger and stronger now, which worried him. So he would hold back. But would she? The determination in her eyes said no. This headgear and these gloves might not be enough to protect him.

"Ready?" She hopped around her end of the ring.

He couldn't help but notice her breasts straining and bouncing against her T-shirt.

Look at her eyes, idiot. This was one woman who couldn't be underestimated, especially in a boxing ring.

"Ready," he said.

She puckered up and gave him an air kiss. "Good luck."

He needed it, because now he was staring at her lips. *Shit.* That woman could kiss. On the stairs. In the hall. Hotter than hell. He swiped at the beads of sweat sliding down his forehead. Did they not have central air in here?

A solid pop to his right jawline woke him up and had him focusing on her smiling face—her whole face.

"A little bit slow today, superstar."

A cheer and some laughter echoed. Great! They had an audience. Of course they had an audience. He always had an audience. He didn't want one now.

"Hey." She bounced back, keeping her hands loose. "I was thinking, what about a celebrity boxing match?"

"Uh, no." Hell, he couldn't even keep up with *her* in the ring.

"Back her into the corner!" some guy yelled.

What? Cam took his eyes off her for only a split second.

She popped him again and smiled. "Yeah, that's probably a terrible idea. I mean who wants to pay to see you get your ass kicked?"

She danced around him, eyes blazing. *Focus, man.*

He managed a jab to her gut before she moved away.

"Thatta way!" the guy cheered.

She approached again. Cam swung. At the last minute, she spun, and his fist hung in midair. More dancing. Little hops. And a rush of laughter. He loved when she had fun. There was nothing more beautiful in the whole world.

She popped him again. Right in the flank.

The guy booed. Cam may have, too, because this didn't seem fair.

"You know, it's okay to hit a girl in here," she said. "I don't want you getting hung up on political correctness and looking like a fool in front of your ... " she glanced at the guy who was watching them, "fan. Singular."

Smart ass. He lunged, and she dodged.

"Come on," she said. "Show me what you've got, superstar."

Oh, he'd show her all right. Just not in here. Later, they were going to finish what they started. He would find someplace where they wouldn't be interrupted by roommates or family members, someplace where they could ...

She bounced to the left and clobbered him. His brain rattled.

The guy gave a disgusted sound, and then walked away.

His one fan had bailed.

Time to stop the insanity. "Okay!" His louder than normal voice halted Tanya in her tracks, but a second later, she was bouncing again.

"What was that?" she asked.

"Just me announcing that the match can finally begin. I think you're good and warmed up." He grinned. "In fact," he bobbed his brows, "you're looking super-hot to me."

Her feet slowed, and her eyes narrowed. "How 'bout from now on you keep your thoughts to yourself? This is a boxing ring, not group therapy."

Yep, he'd unnerved her, and he was just getting started.

"I'm being courteous," he said, shuffling closer and lowering his voice. "I like to let my opponents get a feel for my size before we really get down and dirty." He bit into his cheek to keep from laughing.

"You wish," she said, but she was smiling too.

He advanced. She backpedaled, and then she hit the rope.

"Trapped," he mouthed.

Tanya poked her head around the plastic curtain. "Hey!"

MJ looked at her.

"I get you. I see what you're saying. I'll be careful. I promise." And then she puckered up and blew her a kiss. "Thanks for having my back."

"I have your back too," Jillian said.

"Yeah, to push it right into trouble." Tanya laughed and ducked beneath the warm spray.

"No, not trouble—fun! You can't tell me you wouldn't be grateful if I dragged that fine hunk of man in here and shoved him into the shower with you. I'd even guard the locker room door while you got busy, because I have your back. See?"

Oh, she saw. Her hands dropped over her curves, and her nipples hardened. *That* would be a shower to remember.

More squealing from the stall on her opposite side until the water silenced. "Do you want me to go get him?" Jillian asked.

"No." She laughed. "This isn't high school. I know how to arrange my own booty calls, thank you." She killed the water, wrapped a towel around her, and pushed the curtain aside.

Jillian sucked in an exaggerated breath and held her hands to her heart. "So proud. My baby's all grown up." Then she turned to MJ and tossed her a cocky grin. "You know, she learned that from me." Back to singing that stupid song … *getting busy with good booty.* She held onto her towel as she grooved toward the wall of mirrors, her tattoo of a murderous Cinderella strangling her Prince Charming prominently on display. "Happily ever after" was boring according to Jillian.

Tanya just didn't think happily ever after existed.

MJ's engagement ring flashed as she wound her long brown hair into a bun. In that case, she hoped she was wrong.

"So … " She wedged between MJ and Jillian in front of the mirror and lined up her hair products in order of use. "Enough about me and Cam. What I really need is advice about the gym.

I have 'til noon tomorrow. After that, I don't know if Pop'll wait much longer to accept the offer to sell." Her throat sort of collapsed on the last word. "I'm thinking about taking a personal day tomorrow and going to the bank to see if I can get a loan on my own."

They both faced her, but she continued to look at them in the mirror.

"He won't be happy about you going into debt for him," Jillian said.

"No, but once I sign on the dotted line he won't be able to refuse the money as easily as he can refuse money from Tag or Cam. I'll have it, and I'll have to pay it back no matter what. It'll sort of force his hand."

"Sounds risky." MJ faced the mirror and looked Tanya dead in the eyes. "A lot of risk here, T. You could end up with debt amounting to thirty grand plus interest and still not save the gym. I don't want to sound like a broken record, but please think about this." She patted her back, and then walked away. "I have to go. I told Tag I wouldn't be too late."

When the door swung shut on MJ, a fully clothed Jillian jumped up on the countertop and shook her head. "That ring around her finger has strangled the fun right out of her. She's old and married before she's even old and married. Sad." She huffed and then she wound her blue-tipped hair around her finger and smiled. "I, on the other hand, think it's a great idea. In fact, I think you've been full of great ideas lately." She bobbed her brows. "Where are you going after this?"

Wherever he wanted to go, which was what she'd told him after he'd all but propositioned her in the ring. He had some showing off to do.

She bit back a smile. "None of your business."

"Well, technically it is if you plan to come back to our place. Wouldn't want our booty calls to collide."

Ha! That would be hysterical. She wasn't sure how Cam would react to Jillian's usual suspects—pierced, sullen, and androgynous. "Do you need the apartment tonight?"

"Nope." She grinned. "All yours."

When they finally made it out of the locker room, Cam was leaning against the cement block wall wearing a sinfully clingy T-shirt and baggy sweatpants. He'd showered too. Maybe at the exact time she'd been showering. Her breath caught on the thought of him soapy and naked. Separated by a measly six inches of wall.

"I've been waiting for you," he said. The rumble in his deep voice revved her engines, and she squeezed her thighs together.

Jillian sauntered past him, and then she glanced at Tanya. "Don't forget. I have tickets for Sock Monkey tonight, which is the craziest concert around, so don't expect me home until late—tomorrow." She bobbed her brows. "Use the time wisely."

Subtle, real subtle.

Cam chuckled. "That woman is a piece of work."

Tanya coughed a laugh. "Ya think?"

He placed his hand against the wall beside her head. "So about that thing I said in the ring ... you still interested in a little demonstration?"

The smell of his aftershave was making her dizzy. "Hell yeah."

"Good." He leaned in, so close she could taste him in the air. "You know for a minute I was worried. Thought you might've changed your mind."

Her knees buckled the slightest bit. "Why would you think that?"

"You took a long time in there." His gaze flickered to the locker room door. "So long I would've come in after you if you'd been alone."

She trailed a hand down his front and slipped a finger into his waistband. "I could always go back in."

"Baby, where you lead, I follow."

She pushed her backside against the locker room door and dragged him along by the waistband.

His shirt was over his head before they were safely inside.

Gorgeous. Her fingers traced an erotic path along the deep etches of his traps and delts. *So gorgeous.* A perfect athletic specimen. She knew the dedication required to look like this. All the shoulder presses, lateral raises, and shrugs he had to be doing. A hell of a lot more than he had been doing in high school that was for sure. Because back then, he hadn't looked like this.

The past swirled with the present in her head, making her dizzy. *Pretend he's any man.* Just some sexy lunk who walked into the gym on the one night she happened to be closing.

His lips parted, and he moved in for a kiss.

She dodged it. "This is just sex. No feelings beyond respect for the orgasm and its giver, and if one of us does develop feelings, we take them to the grave. Nobody lays claim. Nobody gets jealous. Either one can walk away without repercussions. We bounce right back to being friends without the benefits."

He gave her a slow, sexy smile. "Do I need to have my lawyer look over that contract before I sign it? Or can we just seal it with a kiss?"

She laughed to humor him, but there would be no kissing. She'd have better control over the situation that way.

"And what if I want to negotiate the terms?" His hands skimmed her hips, then up her waist beneath her shirt. "You know, how often do I get it?"

"Whenever *I* want it. No negotiation. That's the offer. Take it or leave it."

He forced her shirt over her head from the inside out, and pulled her hard against his chest. "I'm going to take it. All of it. And when I'm done, you're going to beg me for more."

●●●

Cam's words sounded strong, but his fingers shook. She stepped back, giving him a long look at her strong upper body and the zipper-front sports bra squeezing her breasts. He swallowed a groan. Cotton had never looked so good.

"Mm, mm. Woman, you slay me." He grabbed hold of the zipper and tugged. Slowly. Anticipation thinned his breaths and hardened his dick. He'd dreamed of this more than a few times after that fumbled night together. The more he'd learned, the more he'd wished he could've shared that capable confident man with her. Then maybe she would've looked at him with something other than friendly indifference afterwards.

Her hands skimmed his abs, and he sucked in a breath.

Friendly indifference was not an acceptable outcome now.

The zipper split, and her breasts swelled. *Damn.* He lifted them to his open mouth, and let his tongue tease until her nipple formed a point. She arched her back, forcing more flesh into his mouth, so he sucked. And she moaned. Which pleasantly surprised him Tanya had never given away her emotions easily. But he seemed to be making short work of the wall tonight.

His ego swelled along with everything else until he was so hard it hurt.

She moaned again when he dragged his mouth to her other breast. Her warm hands sprawled across his head, holding him in place. That hot act of possession made him smile as he licked. There was nothing like the sound of pleasing a woman. Second only to the sound of sixty-eight thousand screaming fans.

He slipped his hands into the waistband of her yoga pants and cupped her ass. Soft and round. Just the way he liked it. His thumbs met with the V of a thong. Excellent.

"Come here," he pulled her by the hand deeper into the locker room. The showers seemed like the logical place, but she pawed at his pants as he walked until the elastic band slipped low on his butt and caught on his erection. He turned and drew her against his chest.

A slow, long, liquefying kiss followed, and when he came up for air, her face was twisted.

Warning bells sounded in his head. "What?" he asked.

She exhaled, and her expression relaxed, but an unsettling blank stare remained.

She was having second thoughts wasn't she? *Damn it.*

"Hey." He stroked her cheeks with his thumbs and was just about to say he understood her hesitation when she gave him a little shove and dropped him to a wooden bench. His breath caught when the cold surface hit his ass, but the rest of him was hotter than field turf on a hundred-degree day. And getting hotter. Because whatever reservations she'd had a second before seemed to have melted away.

"Just sex," she said.

There'd be no complaints from him.

She lifted his sweats and boxers over his penis, down his legs and ditched the bra, leaving her breasts to hang heavy while she worked. He reached out to hold them, tease them, make her moan again.

She lowered on to his lap, ending up with his hardened length in her hands. Her eyes went dark. Her lips parted. But he had the oddest sense that she was holding back.

Not tonight, sweetheart. He reached between them and used his thumb to stroke her slippery center. *Let go. Stop thinking.* Because while she was even bolder and stronger than he remembered, the overthinking part hadn't changed. And right now, he just wanted her to feel.

He teased her with his fingers and leaned forward for another kiss, but she dodged it with a small smile and a faster pace of her hand. This time, he was the one who moaned, and he rode out each wave of pleasure with a clench to his jaw. *Not yet.* Not until she had hers.

"We need a condom," she said even as her pelvis pushed against his hand. "You know what they say about professional athletes. They get around."

It was so abrupt, he stopped and stared at her. "Not this one. Not like that. How 'bout you?"

She palmed his testicles and circled her thumb on his head. At that point, he hardly cared. Stupid, yeah, but he trusted her.

"We're probably safe, but why take chances?" she asked. "Jill has condoms in her locker."

Of course she did.

He watched Tanya cross the room. Bold and bare. Her words echoed in his ears. *Why take chances?* Unlike some of his teammates who had a revolving-door policy, his practice of not sleeping with anyone he wouldn't marry had kept him clean over the years. She couldn't know that, of course, and he didn't know if she was on the pill. An unexpected pregnancy was not what they needed. But still. *Why take chances* sounded like it was just another barrier between them. *Yeah, and you put it there, Buddy.* The hint of mistrust. The fact that she didn't know who he was now or what he'd been doing outside of football. That was his fault.

He was hit by the strongest desire to make up for it.

A gold packet glistened between her fingers as she strode through the locker room without a hint of embarrassment. Confidence was sexier than anything he could think of. She smiled as she returned to her straddled position. "You need help with this?"

You bet he did, but not yet. He had a feeling her push to rush right to the main event came from more than a worry they'd be walked in on.

He slipped a finger inside of her, and she moaned. He used his thumb to circle her nub, and the combination of sensations must have been magic, because she closed her eyes, dropped her head back, and rocked against him. Pure satisfaction. And what a show.

"Come for me, baby," he said.

She froze, but he kept sliding his thumb up and down, and soon she was moving again. Bouncing. Like she'd bounced in the ring. Jiggling her breasts inches from his mouth.

"Come for me," he said again.

Her hands gripped his shoulders. Her nails bit into his skin. Her mouth opened, and she whimpered.

"That's it." He brushed the palm of his free hand over her pointed nipple and opened his mouth to breathe. He was dizzy.

She whimpered again. Louder. Her bouncing became a circling of her hips against his hand. And then her head fell forward and her body bucked against him.

Score. Adrenaline ripped through his body hot and powerful.

He opened his mouth to her shoulder and kissed his way to her neck. "Perfect."

"Not bad." Her soft chuckle vibrated against his lips.

He heard the rip of the condom packet and felt her hands on his erection. He was ready. So ready. He eased his back to the cold wall behind him and let her take control. Watching her was half the turn-on. But she didn't seem interested in watching him. She closed her eyes as he entered her. Maybe that should've bothered him, but it was hard to care when she started moving.

Her slow, easy pulses became quick, hard bounces, shaking him to his core. He gripped her waist and drove up and in. Over and over again. Wanting to climax, but never wanting it to end.

She bit her bottom lip, gripped his shoulders, and snuck the smallest peek. It made him smile, and she surprised him by smiling, too. Finally, those beautiful brown eyes opened wide and locked with his.

He drove into her again. The increased connection ripped the orgasm from deep inside.

He emptied everything he had into her. Went soft. She crumpled too, dropping her cheek to his shoulder on an exhale. *A million times better than last time*, he thought. He smoothed a hand over her bare back to cup her neck and settled in to enjoy the closeness he'd never gotten a chance to experience last time. Under the bleachers hadn't been the most convenient or comfortable place, and the awkwardness between them hadn't helped. He couldn't help but compare. They were more confident now, *and* he had a bench. He smiled as he kissed her neck.

He could stay like this forever.

But all too soon, Tanya stiffened and straightened. "I'd call that redemption," she said. Then she slid off him with a small smile and gathered her clothes. She disappeared behind a row of lockers.

Wait. What? Sure, he'd been having similar thoughts, but the way she just threw it out there and then got up and walked away? Damn, she hadn't been kidding when she'd said just sex.

Talk about anticlimactic.

He roughed a hand over his face. What happened here was more than redemption. He didn't know what to call it, but he knew he wanted to do it again. And again. But if all she felt was vindicated, then he might not get his wish. Nope. That wouldn't fly. He was Cam "damn" Simmons, the Super Bowl MVP. And she wanted him just as much as he wanted her. He'd just have to remind her of that.

Chapter Nine

Tanya had never hyperventilated. Not even during her first playoff game when she lined up opposite a three-hundred-pound woman with a reputation for bone crushing.

She finished straightening her shirt, and then stuck her head inside a random locker to breathe without the risk of being heard.

That man was way more trouble than she'd expected. When her guard was down, the feelings came flooding in. So she tried to temper them. Pretend he was someone else. Limit the kisses. Cut off the cuddling. No matter the distance she put between them. No matter the mind games she tried to play. He still made her feel things beyond the orgasm.

"You looking for something?"

She jerked her head at the sound of his voice and hit the shelf above her. *Son of a bitch.* She groaned.

"Ouch! Are you okay?" He was behind her, rubbing her head and hooking an arm around her waist like he had every right to touch her like that and comfort her like this. Intimate. Caring. Way more than a booty call would do. But that was all this was allowed to be.

So why did she feel like leaning into him and letting him kiss her freaking "booboo"—among other things?

She blinked up at him through watery eyes. "I'm good." *Liar. Liar.*

"Good."

She turned her back to him, picked up her duffle bag and went back to rubbing her burning head. "I just need to sleep it off," she said.

There. The opening to walk out. But her feet didn't move.

His smile softened. "Hasn't a trainer ever told you it isn't good to sleep after you hit your head?" His hand slid to her hip again and his thumb strummed a sexy rhythm on her waist.

Her head felt better. Hell, all of her felt better when he looked at her like this. And so it began again. The desire so deep it scared the hell out of her. The lust so loud she couldn't ignore it.

"Then I guess I shouldn't sleep," she said.

He shook his head and dropped his lips an inch closer to hers. "Someone should keep a very close eye on you for the next twenty-four hours."

She nodded. "Jill is gone."

"Then I'll do it." He kissed her, and she melted.

Mmm. She'd wanted her mouth on his the entire time he'd been touching her, filling her.

Her brain was so fogged over by his kiss that she didn't even bother to look in the mirror before they scrambled out of the locker room and into the empty gym. Overheated and ready for more, she rushed toward the front door, sensing Cam right behind her.

"Hey! I didn't know anyone was still here."

Terrell? Tanya turned to see her brother standing in the doorway to their father's office. "What are you doing here?" she asked.

"Been here. Came in while you two were dancing around in the ring."

One meeting and the guy thought he ran the place. "Listen, I don't know exactly what happened this afternoon, but Pop's not going to sell. I'm going to take care of things once and for all tomorrow."

"How?" Cam asked.

For a split second she'd forgotten he was there. She hesitated. She really didn't want to let him in any more than she already had. And that was kind of laughable, because man, oh man had she let him in. But if she had a shot in hell at keeping this just sex, then she had to draw the line somewhere.

"Don't worry about it," she said.

Hurt flashed in his eyes. "Okay."

Terrell walked toward them. "Well, I have an idea, too. I've been researching fundraising ideas, and I found one that's gonna make a killing. Hands down. You ready for this?"

No. Her going to the bank was the only idea they needed.

"A bachelor auction," he said, and then he let out a whoop. "We'll hold it right here, and have Cam as headliner. How about that?"

What a dumb idea. She opened her mouth to argue, to tell him to leave this to her. She would find a way to save the gym. *He* needed to find a job.

"That could work," Cam said. "I did a bachelor auction a few years ago, and the charity raked in the cash. We had a lot of fun too."

He and Terrell shared a laugh that made her skin bristle. What kind of fun was he talking about here? She cut off that train of thought. Not her business.

She looked at her brother with disgust. "Terrell, I appreciate you trying to help, but this is a gym. A serious gym. There's no way Pop would go for something like that." Her father was as practical as she was. And reputation meant everything. "Just leave it all to me."

"I would, but Pop put me in charge."

Her eyes narrowed. "Of what?"

"The gym." He swung the master set of keys on a lanyard around his neck.

So he *did* run the place? Tanya reached into her pocket for the single front door key her father had given her. Pop really was giving up if he handed everything over to Terrell.

"I don't know what's going on here, but I'm going to talk to him." He may have put his son in charge, but he owned this gym, and his daughter still had a say. And she wasn't ready to give up yet or to turn this place into a meat market.

She stalked toward the front door.

"T, don't be like that," Terrell said. "We can work together."

"Hey, I thought we had plans," Cam said.

Yeah, she'd thought so too. But suddenly she wasn't in the mood. "Another time," she said.

She tramped up the steps to her father's apartment and pounded on the door. No answer. It was too early for him to be in bed, but too late for him to be out. Panic mixed with annoyance, and she turned the knob. Unlocked. Unlike her, the man was awfully trusting.

"Pop!"

No answer again. *What the hell?*

She pulled her phone from her duffle bag and dialed him.

"Hello." He sounded ... sleepy.

"Pop? You okay?"

He cleared his throat and answered, "Yes."

"Where you at? 'Cause I'm at your place, and you aren't here."

"I'm ... at a friend's," he said.

Sleeping at a friend's? Her stomach dropped. *That* kind of friend. Oh God. She didn't want to know this.

"Is everything okay?" he asked.

She shook her head. She didn't have a clue. If he would just step up and take charge again, she'd feel a whole lot better. "I saw Terrell at the gym and he's ... he has some ideas I don't think you would approve of. It's still your gym, Pop. Please don't give up yet. At least be there with Terrell to guide him."

He cleared his throat. "I need a break, Tanya. It's been a long time coming. And I believe in Terrell like I believe in you."

She heard whispering in the background. Definitely a female. The *friend*. She shouldn't have called. "Okay. Fine." For now. "Talk to you later." Tomorrow. After she walked out of the bank with thirty grand in hand. Then everything could go back to the way it had been.

• • •

Friday morning, Cam pulled into the roundabout in front of East High with a carload of teenage girls making more noise than a stadium full of diehard fans during overtime.

"Don't open your doors," Corinne said. "Not yet. Let the anticipation build." She squealed.

He looked at his cousin like she was an alien, then he glanced in the rearview mirror at her three bouncing friends who were just as wired as Corrine.

"Oh my God! Look at Raylee Santana," one of the girls said. "Close your mouth, girl, or you're gonna be catching flies. You know she's like, 'Who is that?'"

Corinne waved a hand over her head. "Oh, she knows who it is. What she's really thinking is, 'I should've been nicer to Rin when I had the chance.'" She snapped, and her friends laughed.

"She's going to be real nice to you now," another girl said.

"Wait! There's Wyatt." Corrine slapped a hand over her mouth and leaned closer to the tinted window. "Deep breath. Okay. On the count of three. We get out, and we don't even look at him. Let him look at me. Ready?"

Cam shook his head. What the hell was going on in here?

"One, two, three."

Commotion. A few "Thanks, Cam"—with extra emphasis on his name. Three doors slammed. And then quiet.

Damn. He could not see himself the father of girls like that. No way. He would raise his daughter to feel as special and powerful walking to school as she did if she showed up in a limousine. It would be about her, not what she had. But that was easy for him to say now that he had what he had.

He parked around back and waited until 8:00 a.m. when the students were in homeroom to enter through the front doors and check in at the office like Coach Pratt had instructed him to do.

"Remember how to get there?" asked the smiling secretary who hadn't been around when he'd been going to school here.

He nodded. "There's not a football player in this school who will ever forget his way to the weight room."

It had been East High tradition for the football team to have weight training first period during the spring semester followed by study hall. It allowed them to stay in shape over the off-season and keep up their grades too. And it had been something Cam always looked forward to. Today was no different. Even though he was attending more for motivation than for a good, hard workout.

He hung a left down a mint green hallway that led in the opposite direction of the stairwell. He had exactly nine minutes before the bell would sound for the end of homeroom. He didn't want to get caught in a swarm of people, but he wanted to see Tanya. Real quick. He just wanted to make sure everything from last night turned out okay. She hadn't been happy with Terrell.

"Hey!" He poked his head around the doorjamb.

The man who had been sitting at Tanya's desk faced him. "Cam Simmons! What can I do for you?"

Cam faltered and looked around the small room like somehow he'd missed her. "I was looking for Tanya Martin."

"Ah. Not in today. I'm Vance Royhill, the sub."

Was she sick? Was something wrong? "Thanks. Sorry to bother you."

He backed out of the room and headed in the direction of the stairs. With his phone in hand, he texted: *Stopped by ur office to say hey. Where u at?*

No answer came by the time he reached the weight room, so he tucked the phone into his jacket pocket and left it inside Coach Pratt's office while he focused on motivating the football team. But in the back of his mind, he wondered why she wasn't in school today.

It was ten o'clock by the time he made it back to his car. The minute he did, he called her cell phone. She didn't answer. She was sick. She had to be. What else could be going on?

He drove the half-mile to her apartment and took the back stairs he only knew existed because she'd lured him up each step with the swing of her hips and the sparkle in her eyes. But that had been nothing compared to last night. He unzipped his jacket on the heat of the memories.

When he reached her apartment, he knocked. But nobody answered. What if she was really sick, so feverish she couldn't get out of bed to answer the door? Her nephew mentioned a key. But that would be weird wouldn't it?

He knocked again. Louder this time. He could always go downstairs and see if Mary or Grace were here.

The door opened, but it wasn't Tanya.

"What's up?" croaked a clearly hung-over Jillian.

"I wanted to see Tanya."

"Not here."

"What do you mean she's not here? She's not at work either."

"Calm down, lover boy. She took the day off, something about going to the bank. But don't hold me to that because I wasn't exactly sober when I came in. Heck, I'm not exactly sober now. But she's fine. And I'm going back to bed."

She shut the door, and he stared at it. *The bank.* Her plan to fix things once and for all at the gym. She was going to borrow money from a bank and pay back interest rather than borrow it from him. *No strings.* He shook his head. That was ridiculous.

He jogged to his truck, determined to stop her, even though he had no idea where she banked. But she was fairly predictable, and she wouldn't put her money outside the neighborhood. In fact, she struck him as a credit union sort of woman, so he swung past the red brick building on French St. first, looking for her lime-green

Kia. He slowed his speed, scanned the cars parallel parked in the street, and then pulled into the lot. Nope.

The only other bank he knew of in South City was Northern Savings & Loan on the corner of Third and Pope, so he hightailed it over there just in time to see her walk out the front doors. Her chin was up. Her strides determined. Her eyes blazed straight ahead. She got the money. He was too late. Or not. He knew her well enough to know a denial wouldn't have resulted in anything less than refusal to be ashamed.

He swung into a spot in front of the bank and rolled down the passenger side window. "Hey!"

She stopped and looked in the direction of his voice. Her face wrinkled, and then she shook her head and walked on.

He jumped out of the car and caught up with her. "Talk to me."

"I don't want to talk to you."

"Why?"

"Because I don't even know why you're here. This doesn't concern you."

"You weren't at school. You didn't answer my texts. I was worried."

She shot him a cold, hard look. "You don't have to worry about me. I do just fine on my own."

His shoulders slumped. "So I take it you got the money."

"Again, it's none of your business."

He cupped her elbow and tugged until she stopped. "Quit being such a hard ass." He smoothed his hand up her arm and rubbed his thumb against the patch of skin peeking out above the collar of her winter coat. "Talk to me." Only this time it was more of a plea. He hated the idea that he was in a position to help someone who wasn't willing to take his help.

She exhaled and her posture softened.

"Thatta girl," he said. His hand moved to her neck, where it warmed her cold skin.

She stared up at him with an unreadable expression on her face. "Looks like we're having a bachelor auction."

She didn't get the money. He tried not to look relieved. But he didn't want her assuming debt or paying interest when his bonus for being name Super Bowl MVP alone was three times what she needed. If worse came to worse, he'd make her see that, strings be damned. But right now, this bachelor auction could be the key to keeping peace.

He grinned. "So you're going to exploit me again?"

"You bet your sweet ass I am." Her gaze narrowed as she licked her lips and eyed him up. "I want you naked in ten. I don't care where. Just someplace we won't get caught. This sucky day might as well suck something good." She rushed a smile. "Are you driving or am I?"

Her grabbed her hand and pulled her toward his car. For once, he was glad his mother was working a double shift.

"I'm warning you right now, I want it quick and dirty."

For some reason, her demand stated on the sidewalk outside a busy bank made him laugh. And to his surprise, she laughed too.

"Get in the car." He held the door open for her.

She stopped with one foot on the running board and wound her hand into the collar of his shirt. "I'm serious. No sweet talk. No cuddling. Quick and dirty."

Hell, just the words on her lips had his blood humming.

"I can handle that," he whispered.

But one of these days, they were going to do it his way.

Chapter Ten

Life was easier when she was sleeping with Cam. He was virtually everywhere she went anyway. Might as well put the boy to use. He was a great release of tension from things like bank loans that were denied due to a lack of sufficient credit history.

The whistle blew, and she plowed into Rosie Gomez. Football helped release tension too.

Coach clapped. "That's what I call blocking, ladies! Good job! Now hydrate, and lose the helmet and pads. I have something fun planned."

Tanya trotted to the sidelines flanked by MJ and Jillian. "Something fun planned? Him?"

"He totally got laid." Jillian pulled her helmet off and dropped it to the ground. "I mean, when was the last time he smiled? Look at him grinning from ear to ear."

Coach was laughing at something Cam said. *Cam.* She'd almost said "no" when he'd asked if he could come tonight. But she'd been weak from orgasm and in need of his help with the bachelor auction. So, here he was, looking sinfully sexy in knee-length basketball shorts and a shirt that moved like second skin over his muscles.

"He definitely got laid," Jillian said.

Yeah, he did. A smile crept across Tanya's face. They'd managed a quickie in his car before practice. *Gotta love tinted windows.*

"He looks happy, doesn't he?" She felt as happy as he looked.

MJ bumped her. "We're talking about Coach. Who are *you* talking about?"

She couldn't hide her smile as they ran back onto the field. To hell with the magic checkbook—the magic orgasm just might save the world.

"Scrimmage," Coach said. He pitched orange, mesh tank tops at random women. "Everybody who gets a pinnie, stand on my right."

He pitched one to Cam. *What?*

The teams separated according to pinnie or no pinnie, and Coach Howl pointed at the defensive line coach. "You're playing too. No pinnie. Ladies and gentlemen, listen up! It's one-hand touch. One! If your hand causes someone to eat turf, it's a fifteen-yard penalty and automatic first down. Got it? This is only going to work if you're civilized. Nobody wants to be the one who tries to prove something and ends up taking out the Super Bowl MVP. Ya hear?"

Chuckles mixed with nods and "Yes, sirs."

"Run the plays we've been practicing. Concentrate on position and execution. This is about precision not power. Most importantly, have fun. You've earned it."

Cam pulled on his pinnie and sidled up beside Tanya. "Your team's going down."

She grinned. "We'll see about that."

His team broke out to an early lead, but only because Tanya's team was caught off guard by a bomb unlike anything they'd ever seen from the back-up quarterback, Lacy Bentz. It wasn't a pretty throw, but a guy like Cam pulled that wobbly ball in and made it look effortless.

Twenty minutes later, things evened out when MJ ran the ball into the end zone. Beneath the good-natured play, Assistant Coach Ray Ross sounded determined to win.

"Trick play," he said to MJ when they were in the huddle again. "Your call."

MJ looked at Jillian and smiled.

The next time the ball snapped, MJ gave the ball to Jillian, but instead of heading up field like everyone else expected the wide receiver to do, Jillian started looking for her passing target.

"Fake reverse," someone yelled.

Cam, who wound up playing defense, made the read and cut towards a sprinting MJ.

Tanya took off too. If she cut between them, he wouldn't have a clear shot at her QB.

"Martin, what the hell are you doing?" Coach yelled.

Playing touch football the way it was meant to be played, positions be damned. Bottom line, if she couldn't get between MJ and Cam, then she'd give Jillian another receiver.

Tanya saw MJ reach the end of her pass pattern, look over her shoulder, and lift her hands just as Cam barreled into view. She glanced back and saw the shadow of the ball on the turf. If she slowed her pace, turned her head, and locked eyes on the ball, she could watch it hit her hands before it dropped into her bread basket. Just. Like. This.

She squeezed the ball to her body, broke right, and fired on all cylinders. *Run. Run. Run. Run.* Her lungs and legs screamed, but she didn't show them any sympathy.

Cam was behind her. She could hear his feet crunching the turf. Jade Wren was closing in too. By now, the whole team was probably in pursuit.

In the split seconds of silence between her breaths, she could feel him getting closer. She didn't dare glance back to see how close. The smallest alteration would impact her speed.

His grunts grew louder. "I got y ... "

She leaped into the end zone, landing in a tuck and roll. Everything hurt. But the cheers helped.

Someone yelled, "Touchdown!" When she opened her eyes Cam was standing over her with a smile and a hand to help her up.

"Nice," he said. "You really are faster than I remember."

Faster? Hell, the speed wasn't what impressed her. What about the agility? "Did I just somersault into the end zone?" she asked MJ.

"Yep."

"That was amazing!" Jillian rushed toward her.

"That was stupid, Martin!" Coach yelled. "Not worth an injury."

"How do you feel?" the trainer asked. "Looked like initial impact was with your head."

"I'm fine. Winded, but fine." Actually, she was better than fine. *That was all offense, baby.*

Who said you couldn't teach old dogs new tricks?

Coach blew his whistle. "Game over. Practice over. See you tomorrow, ladies."

The crowd around her dispersed, leaving only Cam.

"Whose team did you say was going down again?" Tanya asked.

He grinned. "Yeah well, paybacks are a bitch, Martin. Remember that next week when I take you down on the basketball court in front of your students."

She made a sarcastic noise and rolled her eyes. "You wish."

He shook his head. "What I really wish for is a replay of that somersault. I can't believe you did that."

"*That* was the most fun I've ever had on a football field." God, she loved this game.

"It would've had a much different outcome if I hadn't been holding back."

She nodded. "Because you're an elite athlete, and we're just playing around, right?"

"You're elite athletes too. I'm just bigger." He puffed out his chest to prove it.

"Size doesn't scare me." Her gaze dropped to his crotch for a second. "I thought you knew that."

His eyes widened.

She held in a laugh and turned toward the locker room, but before she could get away, he smacked her ass. "Hey!" She spun on him.

"What?" He looked so damn innocent. "You don't smack your teammates on the ass after a good play?" He shrugged. "We do it all the time."

Bend over, baby, was what she wanted to say, but she'd save that for later.

"We need to get you into the end zone more," Jillian said when Tanya caught up with her. "Ask Coach if you can play TE."

A little jolt zipped through her body, but then reason returned. "I'm not a tight end."

"You looked like one today."

She'd felt like one too. What if she could do it again in a real game situation? How would that feel? She let the thought linger. "I like protecting MJ," she said.

"I know, but there are other people who can protect her. Why does it always have to be you?"

Because that was her role in life. It started the day her father moved out. Somebody had to hold the family together. You'd think her brothers would've stepped up. But Terrell was too busy getting in and out of trouble, and Tyler was too busy chasing after girls. So she did it. Every basketball game she'd insisted her mom and dad sit together where she could easily see them when she looked into the crowd. Every single game from middle school on. In those moments, they were whole again. She'd lived for those moments. That's why when it came time for college, she couldn't leave to play somewhere far away, even if it meant playing at a higher level. So she found something else to play. Football.

Even as part of the offense her job was defense. She was comfortable there. But she'd been comfortable flying through the red zone with the ball tucked under her arm too. It was something to think about, but not now. She had a bachelor auction to think about, too.

An hour later at Mama Mary's, she looked around the table at Cam, Jillian, MJ, and Tag. Terrell was the only one missing, but someone had to man the gym now that Pop was on an indefinite hiatus. If anyone could pull off this auction, they could.

"And you think we can get this ready in three weeks?" MJ asked.

Tanya nodded. "We already have the venue. I printed out some signs announcing the gym's one-night closing on Saturday, March 28, and Terrell is going to hang them up so everyone has fair warning." She looked at the notebook in front of her. "Jillian, can the guy who was going to print up T-shirts print up tickets instead? Cam said hundreds of people attended the auction he was in, but most never even bid."

"It's a spectator sport," he said with a laugh.

She could imagine.

"I'm sure he'll do it," Jillian said. "What do we want the tickets to say?"

Tanya passed her the mock-up she'd finished with Cam's help before practice. "I'm going to talk to my mom about donating the booze." It still annoyed the crap out of her that her mother was the reason her father was in this mess in the first place. Some bottles of wine and vodka were the least she could do.

"Cash bar," MJ said. "Keep it simple and easy for me to mix drinks and collect money."

"Sounds good." Tanya had no worries when MJ was involved.

Cam reached across her arm for a nacho chip. The little brush of skin made her smile.

"We should pull out all the stops," said Jillian. "Think Magic Mike."

Cam choked on his chip. When his coughing slowed, he leaned forward to look at Jillian. "This man does not dance, and he sure as hell doesn't wear a thong."

Jillian booed. "You're no fun."

Tanya begged to differ. He was definitely fun. Just not in a flashy, sequined sort of way. "No Magic Mike. This needs to be something my dad is comfortable with."

"And my mom," Cam said. "Let me have my dignity."

"What about other bachelors?" Tag asked.

"We need guys who will bring in serious cash." She glanced at her big-ticket bachelor. "I'll talk to some guys at the gym. Mitchell for sure. A police officer with a famous canine partner has to be worth something. Dante is a firefighter. Rickie is a DJ. They have potential."

"Remember, they have to come up with their own ideas for dates," Cam said. "The bigger the date, the better the bid."

"What's your date?" Jillian asked.

"An all-expenses paid trip to Boston for training camp. Not the whole thing. Just a weekend." He said it like it was no big deal, but the thought of him whisking some woman off to Boston to watch him play football had her stomach rolling.

Jillian whistled. "Can I bid?"

MJ laughed. "If you can afford it."

"No," Tanya said. "Not even if you can afford it. "We're going to man phones in case there are telephone bidders. I also need you to work promo magic and create a Facebook page."

"How much can we expect to bring in from something like this?" MJ asked.

Cam rested elbows to table. "The winning bid for me was fifteen grand."

Tanya's jaw dropped. Who the hell paid fifteen grand for a pseudo date even if it was in the name of charity?

"Who was she?" Tag asked, clearly impressed by the amount.

Tanya wasn't sure she wanted details. Maybe the auction had been how he'd met Sabrina. She'd been working hard these last few days, keeping it light and fun, nice and non-committal. But right now, it didn't feel that way.

"The bidder was seventy, and her husband came with us," Cam said. "It was a blast."

Tanya exhaled. See? Nothing to fear, just a momentary loss of perspective. She didn't care about what happened at the auction with the exception of how much money it brought in. But ... just to save herself the annoyance of watching someone larger-than-life like Sabrina Quick stroll in, she was going to talk to MJ about ways they could vet the bidders.

She'd rather be prepared than be taken by surprise.

• • •

Cam's next week was full of first-period weight training and flirting with Miss Martin in empty halls every chance he could get. And tonight he would take part in East High's annual faculty-student basketball game.

He was getting awfully comfortable around here.

Almost three weeks into his visit home, and he hadn't complained once about being bored. He wasn't harping about his mother's work schedule. He wasn't shoving Boston down her throat. He wasn't even missing football. Well, maybe a little bit. But it was the off-season, so missing football came with the territory. He just kept thinking this was the best off-season he'd ever had.

He looked up at the uncharacteristically sunny early-March sky and ditched his sweatshirt. He hadn't felt like driving all the way across town to work out at the swanky gym his agent had hooked him up with, but he needed more of a workout than tonight's basketball game. So he'd come here. To his old high school track. For the fun of it. For the comfort of it. Because he hadn't run this loop since he'd been home from college on breaks, and that felt like too long.

A few other people were out taking advantage of the beautiful Sunday. He'd tried to get Tanya to join him, but she was busy putting the finishing touches on the event.

"Watch out for the ruts," an old guy called to him. "Wouldn't want your season ruined."

Cam lifted a hand and nodded a thank you for the warning. He moved off the track to stretch. It was in pretty bad shape. The field in the center was more dirt than grass. Heavy snow could trash natural turf, but this was more than that. There had been winters filled with heavy snow back when he'd been playing here, and it didn't look anything like this.

He set out on a light jog, taking in more of the dilapidated surroundings. Something looked funny when he went into the first turn. Where the hell was the goal post?

Cam slowed to a near-walk alongside the man who'd warned him about the ruts. "Excuse me, do you know what happened to the field?" He pointed. "No goal post."

"Hasn't been a goal post in years."

"How do they play without a goal post?"

"They don't play here. Get bussed to the community college."

Home games weren't even at home? That sucked.

He thought about it as he picked up his pace and managed two miles without breaking much of a sweat. Something needed to be done. When he was finished with his run, he pulled out his phone and left a message for his agent.

Between the time he left the track and the time he reached his mother's house, his agent had returned his call and they'd hashed out a plan. He was going to give back to this community that had given so much to him. Tanya would love that. And tonight—after the basketball game—would be the perfect time to tell her.

Chapter Eleven

Cam walked onto the East High basketball court amid cheers. He towered over the other students, but that was the point—their not-so-secret weapon against the faculty. He lined up next to a kid named Sean, who had made it clear in the huddle that the tip was coming to Cam. He didn't have the heart to tell these kids basketball wasn't his thing. He was only here for the fun of it … and for their gym teacher.

On the other side of the mid-court line, former all-city, state champion Tanya Martin stood in the center circle, wearing an East High t-shirt and baggy shorts that looked every bit as enticing as something made of lace.

He smiled until his cheeks hurt. Despite the noise and chaos in the gym, she smiled back at him … and missed the tip. He laughed until the ball came his way. With a leap, he snatched it out of the air and dribbled to the net for a quick layup. His teammates swarmed him before they headed back on defense. High-fives all around.

"I taught you that," Tanya mouthed with an enthusiastic point at her chest.

"I know."

The very next possession, she drained a three-pointer from the top of the key. The crowd oohed and awed. All he could think was, "That's my girl." And just like she'd done in high school, she turned to the stands for the thumbs-up from her mom and dad. His heart swelled.

"Don't let her show you up," one of the kids said.

But when she managed to steal the ball mid-pass and take it to the rim, he knew it was a lost cause. He liked when she showed him up, because then he could watch her.

By the third quarter, the students had figured out that triple teaming Miss Martin was the most effective form of defense, which left Cam with way too much court to cover. He was beat. Wrecked. And having the time of his life.

With one minute left, the teams were separated by four points. Faculty 54. Students 50. Make that 52. Cam hung on the rim for a second as the ball he'd slammed off the backboard swished through the net. The noise turned deafening.

Tanya nodded and gave him a little smirk that seemed to say she was impressed. Hell, he was impressed too.

In the end, that was his last hurrah. Even a flurry of foul shots that put the students on top, 56-55, couldn't sustain a win after she sunk another three-pointer at the buzzer. But nobody seemed to mind. The gym was electric. And for once, he wasn't the athlete everyone wanted to see.

They surrounded her, pulled on her arms and her T-shirt. Jumped up and down and hung on every word. She beamed in the middle of the commotion. Again, his heart puffed up until it literally ached. So much … respect. He'd never met a more talented, determined, independent, beautiful woman. Never.

He hung back, let her soak up the limelight, and after the crowd cleared, he stayed to help the small crew that included Tanya with clean up. It felt easy and natural being here. Places like that were hard to come by with the life he lived. Even his condo in Boston didn't quite feel like his. But this place … this place was a part of him.

Fixing that field was the least he could do.

When they finally left the building, he drove her around back and parked in the empty lot behind the chain link fence that bordered the football field.

She eyed him up suspiciously. "Why are we here?"

"I have a surprise."

"I'm too old to have sex under the bleachers."

He chuckled. "You're never too old for that, but that's not why I brought you out here."

"We can't work out. I ditched my sports bra when I changed."

Really? He raised his brows. "You're not wearing a bra?"

"Of course I am." She unzipped her jacket and lifted her shirt giving him a cleavage-heavy look at red lace.

Damn. He'd never seen her in anything like that. It was all he could do to keep his hands off her now.

She laughed. "You were bound to lose that game. I figured this would be a consolation prize."

"Come here." He reached for her, but she raised her hands to block him.

"Not until you tell me what the surprise is."

Right. He sat back and stared at the space where the missing upright should be. "I'm going to fix this."

"Fix what?"

"The field." He looked at her. "After I worked out here today, I talked to my agent. We're going to redo the whole thing. Turf it too. New scoreboard. Bleachers. Everything."

Her eyes widened. "That's going to cost a fortune."

"Probably." He grinned at her.

She stared at him. Her lips parted as her eyes roamed his face, and the connection with her was so strong he felt his body swaying closer. But then she looked at the field, and her face wrinkled.

Why? What had she thought that shifted the energy and made her look ... afraid?

"The kids will love having home games at home." She glanced at him. "They will *really* love that. And their gym teacher will be able to take them out for class in the fall and spring. Not sure they'll all love that part, but the gym teacher will."

Her cheeks balled up and her eyes sparkled as the energy shifted again. He loved being able to make her face do that.

He took her hand. "Thank you."

The wrinkles returned. "For what?"

There was a mess of feelings swirling inside of him right now. *Be careful, man.* She'd made it clear certain feelings weren't welcome in this friendship. *We take them to the grave,* she'd said. And he'd agreed.

"For showing me a good time while I've been here," he said.

That got a smile, though. "You just want to see the red bra again."

"Absolutely." But it was more than that.

He struggled to name it. Again, the voice in his head warned him against making too much of this. He was just happy. Here. With her. But he couldn't stay. Whatever he was feeling ended there.

She looked away—like she knew what he'd been thinking.

"It's going to be a great field," she finally said.

It was, but a little bit of his happiness had been driven away.

"Does your underwear match?" he asked.

"Yep."

That put his smile back. "Is it a thong?"

"You're going to have to wait until we get back to my place to find out."

Take what you can get, man. Don't be greedy. If this trip home had taught him anything it was that he was already one lucky bastard. Why push it?

. . .

They were spending a little too much time together. That was all. The rush of strong emotion she'd felt when he'd told her his plan for the field was nothing but respect and admiration made extra confusing by how much sex she'd had in the last eleven days. Sometimes twice a day. *That* was not normal for her. *That* was messing with her head. And it was nothing a little distance couldn't cure.

She felt the scruff on his face against her inner thighs, and sighed. Just a little distance. She wasn't going to do anything stupid like walk away … until she didn't have a choice.

Her body bucked when his mouth landed hot and wet on her center. She sighed again as she settled into her mattress.

It was already March. He'd be leaving soon. She needed to cram as much of this into the next three weeks to prepare for the drought that would surely follow—it was going to take damn-near Superman to turn her on after this man.

A thrill shot through her at the tip of his tongue. She whimpered, opened her mouth to release some of the pressure, and decided that starting tomorrow, she would limit herself to sex with Cam every-other-day. It would be the start of weaning herself gradually.

Her alter ego scolded her. *Could we just enjoy the man's mouth while it's on you?*

She smiled. Yeah, she could.

But the next day, when he popped his head around her doorjamb to ask her if she could leave the building during her free period, he had that look on his face. She was actually relieved she couldn't. Today was a no-sex day.

Then practice rolled around, and he showed up there too.

"Defense on the line!" Coach yelled. "Twenty-yard sprint, twenty-yard stride, twenty-yard sprint, twenty-yard stride. All the way down. Set!"

Tanya watched her teammates launch off the line when Coach hollered, "Go!"

Offense would be next. They'd already done it twice before. That was enough to make her legs shaky and her lungs burn, but apparently it wasn't enough to keep her from stealing looks in Cam's direction. He wasn't even breathing hard. *Impressive*. And those calves. *Ridiculous.* And those thighs. *Sinful.* Maybe she could start the every-other-day thing tomorrow.

"Offense on the line!" Coach yelled, and Tanya glanced at the ceiling. *Thank you, God.* Because she couldn't ogle Cam while she was sprinting and striding one hundred yards. "Set!" She crouched, focused on the twenty-yard line, and cleared her head. "Go!"

By the time she finished the drill, yanked off her helmet, and made it back to the huddle, she was brain dead. Her limbs were limp noodles. And she loved it—lived for it. She smiled at MJ, and MJ smiled back.

"Nice work, ladies," Coach said as he motioned for them to gather around. "Make sure you spend some time looking over the playbook tomorrow."

"I can quiz you," Cam said in a low voice behind her.

That could be fun. Maybe she could promise to lose a piece of clothing for every answer she got wrong as long as he lost a piece for every answer she got right. Wait. That would take too long, and she was meeting with Terrell and her father after this.

Back to the original plan. No sex … today.

When the huddle broke, she cut between her coaches and made a beeline for the locker room, a little space and a cold shower would help increase her resolve.

"Martin!" Cam called.

She hesitated. "Yeah?"

"You hungry?"

Always. She faced him.

"How about dinner?" he asked.

"I already have plans."

"Why do I get the feeling you're avoiding me?" He walked to her, glanced around the field house, and then lowered his voice. "Did I do something wrong last night?" He grinned. "Because it sure sounded like I did it right."

She smiled. "I can't complain."

"Good. I was starting to get a complex."

She rolled her eyes. "Big baby. I'm just meeting with my dad and brother. I want to get to the bottom of the financial situation at the gym. We're going to raise all this money and pay the mortgage debt, but I need to know if that's going to be enough."

Cam nodded. "You want me to go with you?"

Why? She wrinkled her face. *No.* That wasn't necessary. He was just the guy she was having sex with. He was also the guy who was being exploited in order to save her father's gym, but that didn't give him a free pass to family dinner. Did it?

"No, you should be home with your mom. You're spending too much time with me."

"Never."

Oh, that made her tense even as warm fuzzies bubbled inside. It was nice to be wanted. It was. But it was temporary.

"Besides," he said. "She's working again."

Cam's mom had worked multiple shifts for as long as Tanya had known him. The hazard of being a single mom. And yet, she didn't have the same financial worries now.

"She works a lot," Tanya said.

"Too much." A concerned frown bent his lips. "She says it makes her happy, but I don't know how."

Maybe that had something to do with why he wanted his mother in Boston. Maybe he was worried about her. Or maybe his frown had more to do with being tired of sitting around an empty house while he was home.

She could feel a change of mind coming on. "So, you're just going to go home and watch TV?"

He nodded. "While I eat cold leftovers."

Okay, maybe that gave him a free pass to family dinner, because it was sad.

"Fine. We're going to Ramsey's," she said. "You're welcome to join us."

"Not Mary's?"

"Nope. I don't want her involved in this conversation. When she's around, my father gets weird."

"Parents," he said.

"Tell me about it." She angled herself toward the locker room door. "So I'll see you there?"

He nodded. "Did you cave because you feel sorry for me not having anything to do tonight? Because if you did, that's sweet."

She rolled her eyes to combat the hiccup in her heart. "I caved because you're nicer to look at than my brother and dad."

Which was easily the truest thing she'd ever said once she was sitting beside her sullen-faced father—and across from Cam—in the quiet, dimly lit restaurant. "I said yes to this meeting because the gym was supposed to be your legacy," Pop said. "But maybe I waited too long to pass over the reins. Maybe it's too late."

"It's not," Tanya said. "The bachelor auction is going to bring in the money we need to pay off the mortgage, and then we will make a plan to grow the business from there."

"We already sold seventy-five tickets," Terrell said. "I deposited almost four grand into the account today."

"That's a long way from thirty grand," Pop said.

Cam intervened, and by the time he was done telling Pop about his bachelor auction experience, her father looked hopeful, and she was certain bringing Cam to dinner had been a great idea.

"See? You don't need to hand over the reins yet," she said.

Pop moved his water glass an inch to the left and patted his silverware. "I want to." He still didn't look up. "It's time. The last week has been … good."

Ugh. That made her think of the night she stormed his apartment only to find him not home, and the phone call that followed. And the *friend.*

"Fine," she said with a nod, not wanting the gory details of why things had been so good.

A waitress approached, saving Tanya from the slim chance that her father would open up without being encouraged.

"Excuse me, sir," the woman said to Cam. "But that table of women near the window is convinced you play football. I'm not much of a fan, so I didn't know. They wanted me to ask."

He looked at Tanya, and then said, "I'm sorry to disappoint them."

The waitress smiled. "And I'm sorry for the interruption."

Surprised and curious, Tanya leaned in when the waitress had gone. "Why'd you do that?"

He shrugged. "You have important things to discuss. I didn't want you guys to have to deal with the intrusion."

Thoughtful. Her gaze lingered a little too long and the air between them heated. She looked at her plate of deep-fried appetizers for a reprieve.

"I'm happy to run the gym," Terrell said.

She looked up and managed not to roll her eyes. "As long as you don't run it into the ground."

"Jesus, sis, your belief in me is crushing."

"Stop," Pop said. "Terrell needs a job. I gave him a job. That's all it is."

"So there's enough coming in to pay him?" She highly doubted that.

"Not exactly."

She rubbed her hands over her face. "Does the gym break even at the end of the month?"

Her father shook his head.

"Not even close," Terrell said.

She gave him a look.

"What? I look at the books now."

A little too late. But she couldn't fault him for that any more than she could fault herself. "Okay, then that's where we need to put our focus, because I firmly believe this bachelor auction is going to bring in at least thirty grand. Now, we have to figure out how to turn a profit going forward."

Pop sighed. "If I knew, I would've been turning one all these years, but it was never about the money for me."

That was one of the things she loved and admired about him. She just wished it hadn't taken such a toll. He looked older than sixty, and that scared her. Maybe it was a good thing for him to hand over the reins after all. She and Terrell could make the decisions that he found so hard to make. Like maybe borrow some money from Tag to update the place and make a real push at increasing membership and turning a profit that would allow them to easily pay back borrowed money.

She glanced at Cam. He'd probably wonder why she didn't ask him. But he was doing enough already. Besides, by the time the gym was back on its feet, he'd be gone. And she wanted it that way. No strings.

She just had to keep reminding herself that.

Chapter Twelve

"Knock her out, Aunt T!"

Tanya took her eye off MJ for a fraction of a millisecond, but it was enough time for MJ to tag her beneath the chin.

Jace was here, and Pop was with him. It was the first time she'd seen her father in the gym since he'd put Terrell in charge.

MJ leaned over the ropes and tapped her gloved hand on Jace's head. "I would've knocked her out if that had been a full-strength uppercut. Put your money on me, kid."

Tanya bumped MJ out of the way with her hip. "She got lucky, because *you* distracted me." She smiled at Jace so he knew she'd been teasing. "What are you guys doing here?"

"Pop's going to teach me to fight."

"To defend," her father said. "He's old enough."

True, but something else was up. Tanya could tell by the way her father stood stiffly with his hands in his pockets.

"You want me to help?" she asked.

"I want *her* to help." Jace pointed at MJ.

Tanya split the ropes and rushed the kid to put him in a playful headlock.

"You're going to warm up first," Pop said. "Ten minutes on the bike."

Jace groaned.

"Come on," MJ said. "The new bike is open. Let's get you on that before someone takes it. The older bikes are harder to pedal."

Jace didn't waste a beat running off after her.

Tanya loosened her gloves and stripped off her headgear. "Hey. What's up?"

Pop nodded. "I just needed to get him out of the house and into something positive."

God, how many times had she heard that said about any number of kids over the years? But her own nephew? A heaviness settled over her, and she frowned.

"Is he getting into trouble?" She hadn't heard anything at school or from other family members.

Her father kept his head turned in the direction of Jace and MJ. "No. And that's the way I want to keep it. I'm going to walk around for a little bit." Off he went, hands still in his pockets, face carefully neutral. Maybe she should walk with him, trying to pry something more out. He seemed to have a lot on his mind. Maybe things weren't going so well between him and his friend this week. But she just stood there.

"Hey." *Cam.* He squeezed her shoulder, and then moved on to her neck. Usually, his touch made her smile, but it was no match for the growing worry she felt as she watched her father walk around the gym he built, the gym he still could lose if this bachelor auction didn't produce.

"My dad's here," she said. "With Jace."

"That's cool." He rubbed her back, and then gave her a hard look. "It's cool, right?"

"Yeah. It is." Whatever had brought her father here, he was here, and that was where he belonged. Like Aunt Grace would say, she didn't need to be borrowing trouble.

"Good. Now, tell me you have nothing planned tonight or tomorrow morning, because I have something planned for you."

"Cam … "

"What? You've been stressed. I want you to have one night with no worries."

Her eyes narrowed. That sounded a lot like something mushy and romantic people in long-term relationships would say.

"Fine." He lowered his lips to her ear. "I want you to be my sex slave for twelve hours. Better?"

"Better." She grinned.

"Good. Then we have plans at eight o'clock. You hear?" He gave her ass a pat. "I'm going to go have some fun with your nephew."

Despite the tiniest hint of warning bells, Tanya joined them after she dumped her sparring gear into her locker. Cam was on the bike beside Jace, challenging him to ride five more minutes. MJ was making fun of how small the bike looked beneath Cam's weight. Pure fun.

"Okay. Grandson, come with me."

Jace hoped off the bike and joined her father.

"That is so cute," MJ said.

It was, and she hoped it was something she would see for years to come, but the move to Chicago was still hanging over the kid's head. It was yet another reason why she and Terrell needed to pay off the debt and stabilize this place—so Jace had someplace cool to hang when he came back to town to visit his dad.

"Cam, my man!"

Tanya turned to see Terrell walking toward them with a striking, familiar-looking blonde.

"I have someone who wants to meet you," Terrell said. "This is the one, the only Katerina Kloss, anchorwoman extraordinaire, and former Miss Ohio. Gotta throw that in there."

He made a cheesy move with his hands, like lights were flashing somewhere, and Tanya rolled her eyes. At her brother. Not at the woman who wanted to meet Cam. She had no reason to do that. Really.

"Wow, that's some introduction!" Katerina grinned at Terrell.

"I'm a fan." He was practically panting.

Disgusting. Tanya glanced at MJ to see if she was taking this all in.

"And I'm a fan of you, Mr. Simmons." Katerina held out a manicured hand.

"Call me Cam."

"Cam." It was breathy and full of admiration.

Oh barf! The woman could be complimentary without going all fangirl.

"Katerina, this is my sister, Tanya, and her friend, MJ," Terrell said.

The woman greeted them with a little less excitement than she'd greeted Cam with, but she was still very nice. Actually, she was flawless. Even her hands were perfect. Soft. Not a single workout-related callus.

Suddenly, Tanya had the urge to invite her into the ring.

"So a bachelor auction," Katerina said. "Tell me all about it, and I'll make sure you get the coverage you need."

Cam was on like a game-time JumboTron. Bright eyes and killer smile.

"How much are you trying to raise?" Katerina asked.

"Thirty grand," Cam said.

"Done." The woman laughed. "I'll write you out the check right now provided you take me to dinner."

Ooh. Ballsy. Normally Tanya admired that, but not when it was directed at her man.

Her man. Where had that come from? He was her friend, and her temporary booty call. That was it. And while this woman was flirting with him, she was also offering publicity that could make the fundraiser a success and save Pop's gym. That was what Tanya needed to be worried about, not whether or not Katerina had the hots for Cam. There was no room for jealousy in this arrangement. No way. She wasn't going to start that crap. She'd been the one to say if either one of them developed feelings, they'd take them to their graves. And she was a woman of her word.

"I'm flattered," Cam said. "But I think a lot of people would be disappointed if we called off the auction now, and a few of them are here. Fellow bachelors, in fact. Let me introduce you."

Tanya watched them walk away, smiling, talking, and sparkling. "Are you going to follow them?" MJ asked.

She shook her head. Katerina Kloss looked good beside him. "That's the kind of woman he's going to end up with, isn't it?" That was the kind of woman he seemed to gravitate to. Both Abigail and Sabrina looked a bit like that.

MJ punched her shoulder. "Don't make me say I told you so."

Hell, no. She laughed, hoping to shake off the icky feelings and spark something she could live with. Something like, "I don't care what that woman does with him as long as she hands him over to me at eight o'clock." She grinned. "We have plans."

• • •

Cam rolled up outside the Ritz-Carlton and watched Tanya for any sign of discomfort. He had to admit, this was a little over the top—even for him. But he was tired of folding his big ole body into tight spaces like the backseat of his car and twin-sized beds. And having sex at his mother's place just wasn't working for him.

"What is this?" Suspicion was written all over her crinkled up face.

"Sex." He grinned. "My way."

"There better be whips and chains in a room up there, because if I walk into roses and champagne, I'm going to … "

He slipped a hand to her thigh and squeezed. "You're going to what?"

She smirked. "Maybe think about not coming here with you next time."

He laughed. "See? I got you hypnotized with this mouth and these hands. I can do whatever I want, and the next twelve hours we're going do things my way."

"We'll see about that." But she wasn't exactly protesting.

He checked in, under an assumed name, and declined help with their overnight bags. When the elevator door slid shut behind them, she backed against the farthest wall.

"So, what exactly is your way?" she asked.

Nervous. He liked that. "You'll see." He kept his hands wrapped around his bag and his eyes on the numbers lighting their way. Let her stew a little. She'd be practically begging by the time they reached the room.

But instead, she was smiling. "You don't have anything planned, do you? You just booked a room because you're sick of squeezing into my small bed or worse, your car. Right?" She poked the ticklish spot on his side. "'Fess up."

He squirmed as he struggled to open the door. But she kept the pressure on and only stopped when she saw the suite.

"Holy shit! This is huge." She stood in the doorway like she was afraid to come in.

He tossed his bag a good four feet to the sofa, and then reached for hers. "I was looking for the biggest bed … and the biggest TV."

She walked in then, roamed the elaborately furnished, white-and-green room with wide eyes that made him smile. "Good God, this view! The lake almost looks like the ocean." Then she faced the television. "Wait a minute. Are we going to watch porn?"

Ha! "Better. College basketball."

"What?"

"UConn."

Her face lit up. "Are you serious?"

He nodded.

Those gorgeous eyes pinned him. "What about the sex?"

"We'll get there." Definitely.

She seemed to think it over. Her head tipped. Her lips curled. "Okay." But she still looked unsure.

What would it take to bring that last bit of wall down?

Forty-five minutes later, they were stuffed with cheeseburgers and fries from room service, and UConn was down by fifteen.

She wiggled out of the crook of his arm and crawled to the end of the bed, blue-jean-covered bottom in the air. "You want another beer?"

He shook his head against the mound of pillows behind him. He really didn't want anything but this. This was … the perfect life. The stuff that dreams were made of.

She sat, stretched for the remote, and turned off the TV. "What *do* you want?" she asked all sultry and sex kitten-like as she crawled back up the king-sized bed.

He smiled. "What do you think?"

She crawled over his legs, settling her bottom right above his knees, and reached for the hem of her shirt.

He grabbed her hand to stop her, and then brought her palm to his lips. "Not yet."

She looked confused.

"My way starts like this." He slid his hands up her arms and pulled her closer to him until they were belly to belly and almost lips to lips. The lemonade she'd been drinking sweetened her breath and made his mouth water.

When he couldn't take it anymore, he cupped her face and pulled her down the last inch.

Like he'd gotten used to these last few weeks, she took control, slipping the tip of her tongue between his lips, and urging him to open wider.

Instead, he rimmed her mouth with his tongue and held her closer, one arm across her butt, the other across her back. Her warm weight sprawled over him. This was how he did it. Slow and long. Like they had all the time in the world.

He smoothed a hand up her back to her neck and angled his head, lifting off the pillows the slightest bit so he could deepen the kiss—at his pace. She responded by shoving her hands beneath the pillows and melting into him.

Mmm. He got lost in the simple pleasure.

He had no idea how much time had passed before she said, "It's hot in here."

They laughed, and it seemed like one sound.

He lifted her up and rolled her to the mattress beside him. So beautiful. And he was so blessed. Propped up on one elbow, he unbuttoned her shirt with his free hand, spreading open the plaid fabric over her warm skin. "Better?"

She looked up at him, but didn't say a word.

He unbuttoned her pants and smoothed a hand over her belly, prolonging every movement, even as he was driving himself crazy with need.

Her breath hitched, but her eyes didn't move.

There were feelings here. More than physical ones. And they were big. But he wasn't going to say it out loud. He wasn't stupid. So he shifted his weight and dropped his mouth to her ear, where he nibbled a bit.

Finally, she reached a hand to the back of his head and made him good and hard with a moan.

"It's still hot," she said.

And between them, it always would be. The question was, what could he do about it?

• • •

He moved in her and above her, and she rose to meet him. Dragging her open mouth down his neck and her fingernails down his back. Squeezing her eyes shut, but unable to block anything out.

This would be the end of it. His way had stripped away more than clothes. And now too much of her wanted too much of him.

Protect this heart. That was the name of the game.

She managed to make it through the night by rolling to the edge of the giant bed the minute he fell into a deep sleep. When the sun came up, she showered and dressed well ahead of him. Room service and SportsCenter filled the space between them. Although, to his credit, Cam didn't seem to sense the shift. Maybe he hadn't felt it. He smiled a lot, talked a lot too. Then again, maybe this was just the way he was the morning after.

That thought caught in her chest. She'd never had a morning after, never allowed herself to indulge like that. Another first with Cam Simmons. Ha! Why did life torture her like this?

After he dropped her off at her apartment and left her with a brain-draining kiss, Tanya lay in bed, staring at the Yadier Molina poster hanging on the ceiling above her bed. Her next bed buddy was going to be a genuine booty call, and he was going to be a baseball player.

She slid her headphones on and fell asleep to Bruno Mars. She woke to bouncing on the end of her bed.

"Somebody didn't get very much sleep last night." Jillian looked ready to burst from excitement.

"I don't want to talk about it."

That did the trick, sucked the enthusiasm right outta her. "Oh." She frowned. "Damn. That bad?"

That good. "Good or bad doesn't matter. He's leaving. Just like last time. God only knows when I'll see him again."

"He's not leaving for another week and a half."

"Why prolong it?"

"Man, you let him get to you, didn't you?"

MJ had told her so.

Tanya's eyes burned. *Bitch, if you cry, I will kill you.*

"So you're walking away before he can," Jillian said. "Are you sure that's what you want to do?"

She nodded. Absolutely. Tonight she would wallow. Tomorrow she would go back to being just friends with Cam.

Chapter Thirteen

After the beep, Cam said, "Good Monday afternoon, Ms. Martin. I'm calling to see if I can give you a ride to practice today." She hadn't been in her office this morning when he'd stopped by after first-period strength training.

A few minutes later, his phone buzzed. But it wasn't Tanya. Katerina Kloss. Again. She'd called three times this morning, and had left one message for him to return her call.

Ugh. He plastered on a smile and said, "Hello."

"Oh, I'm so glad I got a hold of you. Great news! The sports anchor at my station wants a full segment with you. I was thinking the three of us could go out for drinks and come up with an angle."

Drinks made it sound friendlier than what he was comfortable with.

"We have the number-one sportscast with the eighteen- to forty-nine-year-old female demographic. Seems like that hits your target audience for the auction right there," she said.

Bullseye. "Okay." But he was doing this for Tanya and her dad, not in any way shape or form for him.

By the time practice rolled around, Tanya still hadn't called him back. Now, he was officially worried. Was something wrong, or was she dodging him on purpose?

"Hey!" he called out when he saw her hit the turf.

She smiled and waved like he had nothing to worry about. But while he watched her go all out at practice, his doubts grew. Something wasn't right here, and he bet it had something to do with last night. She was scared. Those damn feelings she wanted to take to her grave.

He waited for her outside the locker room even though he'd made plans to watch a movie with his mother and aunts.

Her steps faltered when she saw him. And she was with her bodyguards again. He smiled at MJ and Jillian. "Ladies, nice practice."

They smiled back. Nothing out of the ordinary there.

"Did you drive?" he asked Tanya.

The women exchanged looks, but nobody answered.

That was odd.

Finally, Tanya said, "MJ drove," a little like he'd expect her to say, "Fine. I give up. Shoot me."

What the hell? "Then how 'bout riding with me?" he asked.

Her blink lasted a split second too long.

"Okay." She shuffled toward him.

MJ and Jillian still didn't look certain, so he ushered Tanya away, and he waited until they were inside his car before he asked, "What's going on with you? Or is it me? Did I do something wrong last night?"

She sighed. "You didn't do anything wrong. I just think ... Cam, it's time."

His throat felt thick. "For what?"

"It's time to end the ... extras. Friends first. Friends last. You know?"

He lifted a hand to bang the steering wheel, but stopped mid-air. "Because you have feelings for me? That's it, isn't it?" *Fuck!*

You know, he knew this was coming. Hell, he was leaving in little more than a week, but it still knocked the wind out of him. And he just wanted to hear her say it, to let him know he wasn't crazy for feeling something, too.

She shook her head frantically. "We had rules for a reason, Cam."

"Jesus, just say it, T. It's ridiculous to think two people could be friends and then become lovers and not feel something more than pleasant around each other." He got in her face. "Say you have feelings for me."

She lifted her chin. "Fine. I have feelings for you. How's that? Better?"

No. Worse. Because he'd been over and over it in his head these last two nights, and there wasn't anything he could do about it. His life, his team, and his career were in Boston. Her life, her team, and her career were here.

He hit the wheel.

"We can still be friends," she said.

He didn't want to be friends. He did, but … "What if I started coming back more? It doesn't look like my mother's interested in Boston, and I have projects here now. The field. The work I've been doing with the high school team."

She stared straight ahead. "That would be great, but," she looked at him, "it doesn't change anything between me and you."

He hit the wheel again. "Why?"

"Because we aren't going anywhere. We've taken this as far as we can." She grabbed his hand. "If we push it any further, we could cause some real damage."

He snorted.

"You'll thank me one day," she said. "When you're married with kids."

It was ridiculous. So ridiculous. He pulled his hand away.

Again he wanted to pound the steering wheel. This time he was stopped by his phone buzzing in the cup holder. A second later Katerina Kloss's name lit up the dashboard display.

She couldn't have worse timing.

Tanya stiffened for a split-second, and then gave him the fakest smile. "Go ahead and answer it."

"Only because it's about your dad's gym." He hit a button to answer the call. "Katerina, hey. Let me take this call off speaker phone." It didn't feel right to insert an innocent woman into this.

He glanced at Tanya, who played with her phone or looked out the window like nothing that happened here was a big deal. And that made him angrier.

"Change of plans," Katerina said.

"How so?" It was all he could do not to let his anger spill out onto her.

"Skip can't meet for drinks tomorrow. He can do the next day if you're free."

He glanced at Tanya again. "I'm free." So damn free it was a shame.

"Good. Now, one more thing. I was a little disappointed when he cancelled because, well, I was looking forward to spending the evening with you. And then I got invited to this opening for the new community center Coffee Bean corporate is opening in your neighborhood. It's super last minute, but I thought, 'Hey! Since we're both free.'" She giggled. "Would you be interested in escorting me?"

This was hands down the most ridiculous night of his life.

"I don't know. I … "

"They would love to have an inspirational appearance by someone who grew up in the neighborhood and wants to see it thrive again."

Under the circumstances he couldn't come up with a reasonable way out. "Yeah, yeah. I'll be there." He hung up about a block away from Tanya's apartment, and when he pulled into the lot, she unbuckled.

"Thanks for the ride," she said.

He winced at the way that came out. How ironic. Seriously. How many rides had he given her these past three weeks? And still, after everything, he could honestly answer, "Anytime."

But it was all very *friendly*-like.

He watched her disappear into her mother's restaurant, and pounded the hell out of his steering wheel. As he growled and banged, he imagined the airbag going off. Maybe the blow would knock some sense into him. He was not a desperate, depressed man. He had the world by the ass. Tanya or no Tanya, it was time he remembered that.

She might not want him, but there was no shortage of people who did. It was time to focus on those people, like he'd been doing his whole life—every time he thought about the fact that his father didn't want him.

•••

The next evening, Cam skipped Clash practice for obvious reasons, but he also had a legitimate excuse. He needed to get ready to escort Katerina to the community center opening. His mother wasn't particularly happy he was doing anything that involved Coffee Bean and their "underhanded attempts at getting in good with people just so they can make money." *Such paranoia.* But she was happy to see him in a suit.

He hadn't been dressed up in over a month. In fact, he'd been living like a college kid on leftovers and in workout clothes even off the field and outside of the gym. *Back to the real world, baby.*

He straightened his tie knot and swallowed against the restriction. He splashed his face with cologne and weathered the burn. Then he headed out of the city toward the swanky suburban address Katerina had given him. It would've been so much easier for her to come to him, but this was the proper way to escort someone. Besides, it was good to get out of South City. Katerina's Pepper Pike neighborhood with its perfectly maintained rows of homes reminded him of Boston. He'd been stuck in a rewind of his life so long he'd forgotten how proud he'd been to get out and achieve something like this.

Right about now, he welcomed the reminder.

Ten minutes later, she answered the door dressed in a slinky, gold dress.

"You look amazing," he said.

"Back attcha, big boy." She tapped his lapel with her shiny handbag, and a puff of sweet perfume tickled his nose. "We are going to knock everyone's socks off tonight. They're not going to know what hit them." She hooked her arm around his. "Ready?"

Not really.

She pulled out her phone and moved in closer to him. "Selfie? I have a blog on the station's website. It'll be good publicity."

Suddenly his workout clothes and his mama's tired house looked like the more attractive option. But he was a gentleman who didn't back out of commitments, so he smiled through the goofy photo and then led her to his car.

During the ride, she talked. A lot. An occupational hazard for a T.V. anchorwoman maybe. She didn't let him get a meaningful word in on the ride back into town. But every time he looked at her she was so smoking hot and so damn charismatic he'd have been a fool to mind. He was going to go along for the ride tonight and hope it helped him feel better.

But one glance at the steel and stone community center at the farthest reaches of South City, and all he was feeling was confused. With a block of vacant buildings to its east and west, it was positioned more prominently in the Greenhurst neighborhood. *Hmm.* That seemed odd. Maybe they had plans to develop the rest of the area too.

Katerina led him toward the check-in table. Every few feet someone recognized him, but he didn't recognize anyone as actually being from South City besides him. Something else that made him go *hmm.*

A surprising number of people recognized Katerina before they recognized him, and she ate that up. He fell back a couple steps and watched her work the crowd. She didn't miss him, did she?

He felt a tug on his arm and looked down to see a Sharpie and a napkin being offered to him. "Can I get your autograph?" the man said.

By the time he finished signing, Katerina had disappeared into the crowd. If he hadn't driven her here, he would've cut out. Gone home and curled up on his mother's couch.

A waving on his left caught his attention, and there she was. When she reached him, she pulled him down so she could talk into his ear. "You didn't keep up with me."

"You didn't look like you wanted me to."

"Of course I did, silly." She slinked her arm around his waist and looked up at him with a smile. "There. Joined at the hip. Well, my hip, your thigh, but why quibble?"

Quibble? He laughed and somehow the sound loosened the knot in his chest. If he could manage a few more of those, he'd be feeling halfway normal.

Once they reached their table, he enjoyed two glasses of Hennessy and some small talk with people who were apparently from Katerina's work.

"When do you go back?" a gray-haired man in alarmingly tight leather pants asked.

"About a week." Honestly, right now, he wished it was sooner.

"Katerina should take you to a Cavs game before you leave. They're having one hell of a year."

He nodded, but basketball wasn't his thing. Unless he was with Tanya.

Tight pants tapped Katerina on the shoulder. "You need to take him to the Cavs game."

"Ooh!" Katerina bounced. She looked cute enough doing it. "The station has a box. That's a great idea. Let me text Al." She picked up her phone from the table and started typing.

Was he allowed to say no? *Dummy. Why would you say no?* What else did he have to do for the remainder of his time here?

From there, the evening dragged on. He looked at his watch every fifteen minutes. The fact he was even wearing a watch again felt strange. He needed football to start. That was the great stabilizer in his life. Once he was back on the field with his team, nothing that had happened here would matter. Not even the thing he was trying to forget about the most. Tanya.

"Come on." Katerina put her phone down and grinned up at him. "Tours are about to start."

She grabbed his hand and pulled him along behind her. They saw the indoor tennis court, the swimming pool, and the exercise room. Then, they heard a speech by some guy named Thomas Rowenthal, who said they were proud to serve the people of the Greenhurst neighborhood. *Greenhurst?* Then why the hell was this thing built in South City?

Shit. His family had been right. These companies were buying up property in South City to serve everyone else but the people who lived there. What were they hoping those people would do, move? Slowly that sunk in, and left him nodding. Yep. They were going to force them out or leave them here to rot.

Well, not his mother. It was time to refocus on getting her to Boston.

Chapter Fourteen

"Get up!" Jillian swatted Tanya's behind.

Tanya turned her head to see Jillian and MJ standing beside the bed.

"Get dressed," MJ said.

"I'm tired. Practice was hard."

Jillian grabbed her arm and tugged. "You're depressed. If you were tired, you would sleep it off. Girl, I hear you in here all hours of the night. You aren't sleeping."

"Doc says you need a drink." MJ looked serious enough, but she of all people knew how serious Tanya was about her no-alcohol-during-the-season policy. "Desperate times call for desperate measures. One drink."

"Two would be better," Jillian said.

Ten minutes later Tanya was up and dressed in sweats. The minute she walked into the restaurant below her apartment she saw her mother behind the bar. *Great.*

She turned to her friends. "Did you plan this?"

MJ gave her the raised brow of innocence. "Plan what?"

"Her?" Tanya pointed toward her mother.

Jillian snickered. "So you're not only depressed, now you're paranoid. This is going to take three drinks."

The first margarita went down easier than she expected it to. Her mother didn't harp, and MJ and Jillian didn't badger. They talked about her mother's new hairdo.

"Red makes me feel alive," her mother said.

It made her look like she was on fire, but Tanya swallowed those words with the help of her second drink. When she was halfway to the bottom, Jillian spun her stool around and stared at her.

Here it comes.

"I saw Cam and his mother at the grocery store today. He said he's looking forward to the bachelor auction."

Tanya rolled her eyes. "Good."

Jillian looked at Tanya's mother. "See? I told you. This mood is about a man."

"The hell it is." Tanya attempted a sincere look in her mother's direction, but the booze had one side of her face lagging behind the other. "I don't care about him." At least she hadn't slurred …. Had she? Ooh! They'd liquored her up on purpose.

"Baby girl, I love you, but you are a liar," her mother said. "I saw you coming in and out of here these last few weeks, and up until now your happiness was growing. That man brings out the best in you." She leaned across the bar and grabbed hold of Tanya's face. "That's what love does."

Love? Tanya snorted. She wasn't *in love* with Cam. "This is crazy." She took turns glaring at all three of them. "Women don't need men to bring out the best in them. I bring out the best in myself." She wiped a bit of spittle from her chin. Okay, so she brought out the worst in herself, too, but that was her prerogative. "Are you telling me Pop brought out the best in you?"

"You're damn straight he did," her mother said. "He still does. He made me a mother and encouraged me to open this restaurant." Tears welled in her eyes. "I wouldn't be who I am today without him."

And that wasn't healthy. That dependency could cost Pop the gym.

"What a crock of shit!" Tanya pushed her drink away and dropped feet to the floor, but she couldn't get off the stool. MJ and Jillian held her in place.

"Don't go," MJ said. "Please."

"Why would I want to stay here and listen to relationship advice from my mother who is divorced, never remarried, and has put my father's dream in jeopardy to further her own?"

Damn. Who said that? Not her. She'd never spoken like that in front of either one of her parents.

Hurt deepened the color of her mother's face.

"I'm sorry." So sorry. She loved her parents to death. She just wished there was an easier way to talk about this. But the truth was, she was bitter. Her mother walked away to take care of someone at the other end of the bar.

Tanya wilted. "I'm a horrible person."

Jillian threw an arm around her. "No, you're just feeling horrible. There's a big difference."

She dragged her drink closer and finished it off.

When her mother returned, she dropped elbows to the bar and leaned in. "I did not make your father hand over any money to me. Ever. I refused more than once. But you know what he said to me? He said, 'Mary, my gym may have cost us a peaceful marriage, but it's going to save your restaurant.' And then he said, 'We'll call it even.'" She shook her head as tears formed. "You're a smart, strong, independent woman, but you don't know everything, and sometimes you can be too damn strong. There's got to be balance in life. And I'll tell you another thing. I was the one who told him not to sell that place, because it's you kids' legacy. I told him to believe in what you and Terrell could do."

Did that fix things? Maybe. Probably. She didn't know. The booze. She was just about to hug her and apologize again when her mother said, "I wasn't going to tell you this part, but … do you know the last time I had sex?"

Tanya recoiled. "No, and I don't want to know."

"Two nights ago."

She felt a dry heave coming on.

"You know who with?"

She plugged her ears, but MJ and Jillian pulled her fingers free. "Your father."

Tanya was so surprised she forgot to gag. Her mother was her father's friend with benefits? This whole damn thing was ludicrous.

"That man was, is, and will always be my soul mate. That's the only way I can explain how we've behaved these last sixteen years. My point is, love is crazy, complicated, and worth every up and down."

"True that," MJ said with a wiggle of her fingers and a glance at her engagement ring.

Tanya was transfixed by the bling and rendered speechless by her mother's words.

"Baby, you have this idea that love hurts, and it can … it does." Her mother smoothed a hand over Tanya's. "But it also feels good, safe, and right, because it's what we're on this earth to do. Don't deprive yourself of that because you're scared you'll end up like your father and me or Tyler and Marissa. You should be so lucky to end up like your father and me." The tears returned. "We might not be orthodox, but we love each other."

Tanya slid her hands away. "Okay. Fine. Maybe you and Pop are this lovey-dovey anomaly, but don't talk to me about Tyler and Marissa. They're ruining Jace's life. Even Pop is worried about him. That's why he's had him at the gym."

"Wrong again, baby girl. You need to talk to your brother about what's really going on with that divorce, because Marissa asked him to go to marriage counseling one last time, and he's agreed. That's why your father has been bringing Jace to the gym."

Holy shit. Her head was spinning. Probably in part to the booze. But her mother's revelations didn't help. Heavy stuff. Then again, what did it matter to her?

It was all well and good that her marriage-challenged family was finally getting their crap together, but that didn't have anything to do with her and Cam. Not really. Sure, she'd grown attached to him over the last month. Yeah, she was jealous—green from the inside out—at the thought of him with Katerina, the woman whose arms she'd practically pushed him into. But attachment and jealousy did not equal a love affair. In fact, they sounded like the beginnings of a mentally unstable relationship.

Love. God, just the thought of the word had her crinkling her nose. It was such a warped ideal.

"I'll have another." She tapped her glass.

After all this, she was damn well going to sleep.

God only knew how many hours later, Tanya woke with a headache. She welcomed it, because when her head hurt like this, her heart hurt much less.

Jillian knocked on the door jamb. "We're leaving in forty-five minutes." She set a cup of steaming coffee on Tanya's bedside table and patted her arm.

But it was Sunday, her day off.

"MJ is talking about body image and women's rights at the Unitarian church today. Remember?"

Not if it came up last night after her third drink. She groaned.

"I know, but the coffee will help."

Not as much as the shower. After that, Tanya felt human again.

They managed the drive across town without a single word about last night's relationship intervention. Tanya mostly stared out the window while Jillian sang along with the radio. When they pulled into the parking lot, a few teammates were hanging outside the church's double doors. Relief washed over Tanya. Talking about what happened last night definitely wouldn't happen now.

More teammates were waiting in the lobby. She loved how they supported each other. This was more important than some temporary love affair. This was damn near family.

"She's going to be so happy to see you all." Tag worked his way into the crowd of women. "She's used to speaking in front of teenagers, but adults make her nervous. Seeing your faces is going to help big time. I had the usher reserve two rows. Just tell him you're with the team." He was beaming.

"That woman hit the man jackpot with him," Jillian whispered.

Yep, Doc was something else, but ... Tanya waited for the cynicism to kick in. Oh, why bother? Her parents were still sleeping together. Why couldn't MJ and Tag have as many years of wedded bliss? Apparently stranger things could and did happen.

When Tag was the first one on his feet after MJ's talk ended, Tanya thought without a hint of sarcasm, *that marriage is going to stick*. She didn't even quantify it with an, "I hope so."

"Let me treat you ladies to lunch," Tag said as the four of them stood outside the church long after the crowd had thinned.

He let MJ pick, and she chose an Italian restaurant in University Heights. A table was already set for them when they arrived. A bottle of sparkling grape juice was chilling in a bucket, and a bouquet of flowers covered one of the place settings.

MJ squealed. "How did you know I was going to pick Geraci's?" She threw her arms around him.

"I know my girl."

Geez. That was impressive. She'd known MJ longer than Tag had, but she couldn't have predicted the restaurant MJ would've chosen with that much certainty.

They kissed, and Tanya looked away. She was happy for them.

All through lunch, Tanya focused on them. So this was what love looked like.

Tag teased MJ, and she teased right back. They exchanged meaningful glances between bites. Then he touched her. First, her shoulder, then he slipped his hand over her back and up again to her neck. MJ's head rolled ever so slightly with his massage.

Tanya felt the ghost of Cam. They'd been like that. Sans the honking rock on her left ring finger and the shared accommodations. They'd been just like that. In sync. In tune. In love.

Her mother had been right.

"Excuse me." She bolted from the table and hid inside the ladies room.

Girl, you better get a grip. Just because she loved him didn't mean she needed to fall apart.

"You okay?" The door swung shut behind Jillian. "Greasy food can be a blessing and curse after a night of drinking. Oh … " Her eyes widened as she took in Tanya's face. "You're not sick are you?"

Tanya shook her head. But she felt sick, because the words, "I love him," were wreaking havoc on her insides.

Jillian hugged her. "What are we going to do with you?"

"Even if I do … " *Say it. Get it out. You'll feel better then*, "love him, and he loves me, what then?" She broke free of Jillian's arms. "I'm here. My job, my team, my family. All here. I want to be here, but he wants to be there."

"Why can't you go there when you can, and he can come here when he can?"

It sounded so simple. "But … but … most relationships are doomed already. Long-distance relationships are the worst. It can't work."

"It can if the people involved are independent and secure outside the relationship."

Tanya made a face. "What the hell do you know about relationships like that?"

"My dad was military," Jillian said. "He missed huge chunks of my life, but I'll tell you what, he was as close as a man could be to my mother. Once, they didn't see each other for a year, but the minute he got home, they picked up right where they left off. My point is, if you love Cam, then you should be with him as much as you can. End of story."

Okay, now that actually sounded reasonable. But part of her was still screaming, "Where's the catch?" There had to be some doom and gloom she needed to prepare for. What the hell was she supposed to do with herself if she wasn't preparing and defending?

"I don't know what to think or do anymore," she said.

"How 'bout you start by calling him and telling him you're sorry for pushing him away these last few days?"

Maybe. She considered it on the ride home. She even pulled out her phone to call him, but then she decided to go to the gym first. Her thoughts were always clearer at the end of a hard workout. If calling him still made sense afterwards, she'd do it.

The first thing she saw when she walked into the gym was Jace shadow boxing inside the ring. Seeing the kid brought back everything her mother had said last night. Tyler and Marissa wanted to reconcile, which meant Chicago could end up nothing more than a close call. The tension she'd been holding in her chest lightened.

Pop climbed into the ring and adjusted Jace's stance. Her mother and father were having sex. Of all the crazy things. Tanya laughed.

Someone else was laughing too. In a blink, the tension returned. She looked toward the sound and saw Katerina Kloss throwing off-balanced punches at the hanging bag while light from a video camera lit her up like a downtown bus stop. Cam was standing right behind her. He squared her shoulders with his hands, and Tanya flinched. *Son of a bitch.* With the camera in plain sight it was obviously publicity, but seeing them having fun together made her heart hurt.

She refocused on her family. Maybe she'd climb into the ring, mess around with Jace, and move the hell on. But the burning wouldn't stop. Neither would Katerina's laughter.

Tanya looked their way again, and this time Cam was looking at her. He smiled. She managed to nod. The pain split her in two. Half wanted to go to him. The other half wanted to leave. And in the space between was the truth. Because she loved him, they could never be *just friends* again.

What do you want, Tanya?

"Him," she whispered. And deep down she knew it wasn't too late to get him.

The problem was, she wasn't willing to take a risk like that without a damn good plan.

Chapter Fifteen

Cam couldn't sleep. He padded through his mother's quiet house to the fridge and opened a plastic container of leftover mashed potatoes. He ate them cold.

The microwave clock read *11:35*. No wonder he couldn't sleep. It was still so damn early. Katerina had invited him back to her place to look at the raw outtakes from the interview they'd recorded earlier that day at the gym. Maybe he should've gone with her, but why lead her on? It wasn't going happen. It was bad enough she kept stringing him along with one publicity opportunity after the other. Like the orchestrated boxing lesson she'd wanted to catch on tape after the interview.

He might not be able to sleep, but he was tired—tired of all of it.

The bolt lock on the back door turned, and his mother walked in from her night shift.

"Baby, you're home." She looked surprised.

He smiled as she kissed the top of his head and lifted the plastic container of potatoes.

"They're cold," she said. "Why didn't you heat it up?"

"Too tired."

"Then why aren't you sleeping?" She plopped onto the chair beside him and gave him a good hard look. "You okay?"

He nodded.

Her nose wrinkled. "You might be all grown up, but I can still tell when you're bothered." She patted his hand. "Is something going on with the team back in Boston?"

"Nope. Everything in Boston is great." Here was his window of opportunity. "Speaking of Boston, I want you to give some more thought to moving."

She threw up her hands. "How many times do I have to tell you I like where I am?"

"Yeah, well this place is only going to get worse with places like Coffee Bean moving in."

Her face twisted with confusion. "That's what I always say, while you say I'm overreacting."

"Let's just say I changed my mind, and I think you should move. You'll like it in Boston, too. I promise. I talked to a real estate agent about the perfect house, one with an ocean view. I know how much you love the water. I saw how your face lit up in Hawaii. Why wouldn't you want to look at something that awesome all the time?"

She looked around the kitchen, and tears formed in her eyes. "Baby, the ocean is wonderful to visit, but this is my home. I bought it with the money I earned." She tapped her chest. "There's pride in that. And the memories! They're all around me." She pointed behind her. "I can't open that door without thinking back to the day I opened it to take you to your first day of school."

Ha! He remembered that too. Not the door-opening part, but bits and pieces from the day. Walking down the sidewalk acting cool in new sneakers, feeling sick when he hugged her goodbye at the edge of the school playground, and then coming home to chocolate cake. He smiled.

"The company I work for might not be as flashy as your companies in Boston, but it also hasn't sold out to a bigger hospital system. For crying out loud, Cameron, the CEO knows me by name."

"Ma, everybody knows you by name." She'd been interviewed numerous times over the course of his career by people who wanted the story of the little woman behind the big man.

"Helen Eckert isn't a football fan. *I* had to tell her who you were, and that was long after she knew who I was." She grinned.

"My point is sometimes it's better to have heart and soul than it is to be flashy and carry a fat wallet."

Yeah, yeah, yeah. It sounded like their conversation at the mall, and a little like Tanya's comment that he couldn't solve the world's problems with a magic checkbook and the Lombardi Trophy. He got that now. Big time. Money only took you so far.

Still, the fact that his mother lived in this house with minimal updating seemed crazy.

"Eventually, you are going to have to do something to this house," he said. "Replace the wallpaper at least. Toss the yellow toilet. Fix the roof."

"When I have the time and the money to hire someone I trust."

"Let me do it for you."

"No."

There was stubborn and then there was *stubborn*. Why didn't she want things to change? "I don't understand you," he said.

"I don't expect you to—not until you have kids of your own."

"So you're saying this has something to do with me."

Her lips formed a straight line.

"What?" he asked. "Tell me. I want to know."

She shook her head. "It's not important."

"It is to me. And maybe it will help me get off your back."

A small smile curved her lips, but then her brows bunched above her nose. Silence. Enough that he thought he'd lost the battle, but then she sighed and said, "He came once. Looking for you."

Cam's heart lodged in his throat. He didn't need to ask who "he" was. He knew.

"You were already in Florida," she said. "I'd moved you into the dorm a couple weeks before he showed up on the front porch. He said a lot of things I'd waited a lot of years to hear, and for a little while I thought, 'Praise Jesus, my baby is going to have the father he deserves.' But then he said something I couldn't get outta my ears. Still can't. He said, 'How much did they give 'em to play?' And I knew right there, he wasn't here for you. He was here for the money you would make. I told him you didn't make anything playing college football, and he said he should've figured that out by looking at the hell hole I was living in. My ship would come in one day, he said. And then the sorry son of a bitch left. Never saw him again. But all these years, I've expected to. I figured he'd want me to lead him to you." His mother placed a hand on his cheek. "And that ain't gonna happen."

Stunned. Like he'd been blindsided in the middle of a catch. All these years. All the ideas he'd had about where his father was and why he stayed away. Slowly the confusion cleared. "You think moving to Boston, where I am, will lead him to me?" he asked.

"Maybe. But it's more than that. Cameron, as long as you are my son, showering me with gifts, I've got to be careful trusting a man. Is it me he wants or is it the mother of a professional football player?"

Damn. He collapsed back in the chair and tipped his face to the ceiling. "I'm sorry. I had no idea this would be so hard on you."

"It's not," she said. "Don't say that. Seeing you succeed has been a blessing. I just don't like when you push me to be someone I'm not, but I know you mean well." She covered his hands with hers. "I love you with every fiber of my being, but I hope now you can see that following you to Boston would be a mistake. That's your life, baby, not mine."

He nodded. "You're right." And if it weren't for this bachelor auction, he'd leave tonight. Reclaim his life. Let everyone get on with theirs.

"I usually am." She smiled. "I'm glad we finally had this talk."

He couldn't say the same. Not yet. Right now, he was sad, angry, and a little confused. Where was his father now that it was obvious Cam had money? Not that he wanted to be played and used.

Shit. He was a mess. He didn't know what he wanted beyond the football season to start again—and Tanya. He couldn't stop thinking about her.

"You know what else I'm glad about? Even though your life is in Boston, you're finally making room for Cleveland. What you're doing for Pop Martin is wonderful. And I overheard your telephone conversation about turfing the high school field. That's the stuff that shows what you're really made of. The true measure of a man. It's how much you give, not how much you earn."

She was making more out of it than it was. He had money. He spent it. Occasionally he did something good with it. But he was no Pop Martin. That guy gave practically everything he had, and he didn't have anywhere near a magic checkbook. He had heart and soul though, and that seemed to be enough.

Tanya was a chip off the old block. She had heart and soul like her dad. And now she had Cam's heart too. Because he loved her. He knew it the minute he saw her in the gym.

That's why he hurt so bad.

"Thanks for the chat," he said. "It … helped."

"Good." She stood up, pushed in her chair, and kissed him on the head.

He watched her lock up and turn the back light off. "I'm going to be heading back to Boston a little early," he said. There was really no reason for him to stick around. "After the auction." The winner would be bidding on a trip to Boston, so he wouldn't have to wait here to fulfill the date.

She nodded.

Damn guilt. After everything that had happened, he didn't understand why it was still plaguing him. "I'm starting to feel … anxious about the season," he said.

"I'm sure you are." She patted his back on her way to the living room. "Sleep tight, my boy. I need to get some rest too. Double shift tomorrow."

He lingered in the kitchen after she'd gone. In the stillness, he stared at the back door and let the memories rush in. Maybe it wasn't popular or practical, but he was glad she hadn't changed much. This was his home. The only other place he'd ever felt this comfortable was on the football field. His house in Boston and his condo at the beach were impressive, but lacking somehow. *No heart and soul.* But no connection to Tanya Martin either. And right now, that was what he needed.

He looked at the same wall calendar he'd stared at when he'd arrived in town. Just a few days until the bachelor auction. Then he could put everything else behind him.

• • •

The night of the auction turned cold with lake effect snow threatening to keep people home. If the three feet they were predicting fell, it would certainly keep Cam in Cleveland another day. *Hell yeah. Why don't we prolong the torture?* He slammed his locker, pulled on the silly satin boxing robe, and collapsed on a nearby wooden bench. He looked like a freak and felt like a fraud. Then it dawned on him. The last time he'd sat on a bench like this it was in the women's locker room … while Tanya sat on him.

Cam hung his head. His SUV was a four-wheel-drive. Three feet of snow wasn't going to stop him.

The door opened, and he looked up. For a split second he wished to see Tanya. Maybe she'd been obsessing over him the way he'd been obsessing over her.

But it was Mitchell. Of course it was Mitchell. Tanya couldn't even look at him. She was damned determined to take whatever she was feeling to the grave. What a joke! What did that prove? The no feelings rule was supposed to preserve their friendship. Look how that went. *Hypocrite!*

Anger straightened his spine until he was standing. She shouldn't get away with that. If their friendship was done, then what did he have to lose by telling her how much he really felt?

How much time did he have before the auction started?

The door swung open again. "Press," said a familiar voice. "I hope everyone is decent." Even if he hadn't recognized the voice, he would've recognized the laugh.

Katerina.

Ugh. He wished there was an escape hatch.

She took one look at him and said, "Be still my beating heart." Her trusty camera crew tagged along.

He rushed a smile, and then ducked behind a locker door.

She tugged on the belt wrapped loosely around his waist. "These outfits are so cute. Whose idea were they?"

He leaned into the locker and pretended to search for something. "Jillian Bell's." His voice echoed against the metal walls.

"For the camera, silly."

There had to be some way out of this. He didn't want to be interviewed. He wanted to find Tanya.

"Toss me that sneaker," Mitchell said in the distance.

Mitchell! Cam looked at Katerina. "Can you give me a few minutes? Go interview Mitchell first. You know Officer Mitchell Grant, right?"

Katerina's eyes widened, and then she glanced over her shoulder. "Yes! We did a three-part series on him and the canine unit last year." She gestured to the camera crew. "This will be a great follow-up. We'll be right back."

Excellent. By then he wouldn't be here.

When her back was turned, he slipped into the hall and saw Terrell. "Have you seen Tanya?"

Terrell shook his head. "Nah, man. I haven't been up front. I'm making sure the lighting guys have everything they need."

So she was upfront. He made his way to the partitioned section behind the ring-turned-stage.

Pop smiled at him. "Looking dapper."

Cam glanced down at the ridiculous outfit and laughed. "Thanks."

"No, thank you." Pop smacked him on the back. "These people are here because of you. If this works, I'm going to have to rename the gym."

Cam hesitated. He didn't want to be given that much credit. "These people are here for you." Hell, this whole damn section of town should be named after this man. Getting the people in power to agree to that might be a stretch but … what about the new high school football field? Cam warmed at the thought.

"I don't think that pretty anchorwoman would be carrying around a cashier's check for ten grand if she had to bid on me." Pop said.

The warmth vanished. Katerina brought ten thousand dollars to buy a date with him. It had to be another publicity stunt, but holy hell! This one was huge. How was he going to get out of it?

He had to find Tanya now. If Katerina won the bidding, he knew exactly how that would look.

"Have you seen your daughter?"

"Last time I saw her she was helping MJ behind the bar."

Cam thanked the man and rushed to the split in the curtain.

"Whoa, cowboy. You can't go out there dressed like that." Some woman he didn't recognize blocked his exit. "No glimpses of the merchandise before the auction."

"There's someone I have to talk to. It's important."

"Call her."

"There you are!" Katerina latched onto his arm.

"Well look at that," the exit-blocker said. "You found her."

"You were looking for me? Why were you looking for me out there?" She laughed. "Come on. You owe me an interview."

Shit. Shit. Shit. Maybe he could talk her out of bidding.

"We're going to raise big money for your gym, Mr. Martin." Katerina shot Pop a smile and a thumbs up. "I promise."

Great. Now, he felt like an ass. What if he talked her out of bidding and nobody else's bid came close. Ten grand? With six bachelors, hearty ticket sales and an open bar, that would surely put them over the goal mark.

"Right here." She maneuvered him so his back was to the cinder block wall in the hallway. "Now, smile. You look scared to death. Where's my million-dollar media baby?"

He grew up. Finally. It was about damn time he figured out what was important, and it wasn't attention like this.

The red light on the camera glowed. "Whose idea was it for the participants to wear traditional boxing attire?"

"Jillian Bell's."

Katerina raised a hand and the red light went off. "Cam, you know how this works. Smile. And for heaven's sake give me more than two words."

"I can't do this right now."

What would it prove? Who would it serve? By the time it aired the auction would be over.

He had to find Tanya.

Loud shushes carried into the hallway. "The MC is taking the stage."

"You're right." Katerina smoothed a hand down his robe. "We're out of time. For now." She winked. "Hope you bring in the big bucks."

His stomach turned. "Katerina, wait."

She turned back to him with a smile.

"Bachelors to your places!" someone yelled.

"We'll talk later," she said.

His phone. If he could get to his phone, he could text Tanya. He lunged for the locker room door.

The door swung open and Mitchell walked out. "It's show time, brother."

"Ladies and Gentleman, thank you for joining us for this important evening!" The MC's voice echoed down the hall.

He was screwed.

Chapter Sixteen

Here we go.

The first bachelor was on the block. Tanya's father stood on her right wearing a stone-cold expression. So much was riding on this.

"Please, Lord Jesus, let this work," her mother said.

Tanya was too nervous and too anxious about seeing Cam go up for grabs she didn't care that technically her mother got them into this mess in the first place. She linked arms with her parents.

Katerina Kloss and her ever-present cameraman moved to an open spot a few feet away from them. Tanya pretended she didn't recognize her, but the woman smiled and waved. *Busted.* Tanya waved back. To her surprise, her father waved too.

Katerina winked at him.

Great. Now her father was sweet on the former Miss Ohio.

"What was that about?" She side-eyed her father.

"Probably has something to do with the ten thousand-dollar cashier's check she showed me. She's got her eye on Cam, and that's gonna help save my gym."

It wasn't anything she didn't already suspect, but hearing Katerina was going hard after Cam flipped a switch inside Tanya. She growled. Cam had been hers first—literally, figuratively, and every-ly in between. She'd been a complete idiot to step aside and leave an unobstructed path to him. Plan or no plan, she had to find a way to intervene.

Her mother vise-gripped her arm. "Maybe someone will outbid her."

The room was filled with well-dressed, middle-aged women clutching numbered paddles to their chests. Any one of them would be a better date than a former Miss Ohio who may or may not be sampling the goods already. Wait a minute. That didn't make any sense. Who pays ten thousand dollars for a date with a man you're already sleeping with? Her breath caught. They *weren't* sleeping together—at least not yet. But if Katerina won the destination date, she'd be whisked off to Boston, given tickets to training camp, and wined and dined by Cam. Two attractive, single people would be sleeping together after that.

Crap. Tanya needed a magic checkbook. If she had one, she'd fake it as a phone bidder and outbid Katerina all by herself just to throw a wrench in the plan.

The crowd around her cheered as the auctioneer said, "Let's open bids for Dr. Landry Powell and his private sailboating lessons at five hundred dollars. Five hundred dollars in front. Do I hear six hundred?"

In a blink, the number jumped to fifteen hundred dollars. There was a flurry of activity all around her while Dr. Powell preened onstage.

Tanya's skin felt clammy, her mouth dry, and her heat thrummed a shallow beat. If she had to stand here and watch Katerina win a date with Cam, she was going to be sick.

"I'll be back." She broke free from her parents and weaved through the crowd to the back of the gym, where MJ was manning the bar.

"What's up?" MJ poured wine into a plastic glass and passed it off to another woman.

Tanya waited until the woman had gone to say, "I needed some distance."

"From?"

The auctioneer shouted, "Sold to the woman in red for three thousand dollars!"

One bachelor down. Six to go.

Tanya eyed up the liquor bottles. Maybe all she needed was a drink. "It's too chaotic closer to the stage."

"Our next bachelor … " The crowd's roar drowned out the auctioneer.

"Mitchell," MJ said. "Dang, they haven't even gotten to Cam. Can you even imagine it then?"

Nope. She might have to escape to the street.

"Wait!" MJ said. "This little visit is about Cam isn't it? I can tell by your face."

She could deny it, but her face would probably give her away again. She leaned closer. "Katerina's going to bid on him."

"She told you that?"

"She showed my father a ten-thousand-dollar cashier's check."

MJ's nose wrinkled. "That seems dumb. What if half that is all she needs to win?"

Katerina didn't strike Tanya as the kind of woman who did anything halfway. "I think she'll wait until the last minute and then obliterate everyone else by dropping the ten-thousand-dollar bomb. The cameras will probably be rolling when she does it."

MJ nodded. "What do you think she wants more: the date with Cam or the publicity?"

"I don't know, but I wish I could figure out a way to rob her of both without screwing over my dad. I mean if I somehow warn Katerina off, there's no guarantee anyone else would be willing to bid ten grand."

Tanya was willing. She just didn't have it. Maybe she could sell something. Her car?

Bitch, don't be stupid.

She was just going to have to let this play out, and then tell him she loved him afterward and hope it was enough.

Tag slipped behind the bar and placed a hand on his fiancée's back. "Landry is happy with the bid, but a little nervous about the bidder. After she won, she jumped onto the stage and kissed him."

God, she did not want to witness a scene like that between Katerina and Cam. Outside was looking better and better … until someone walked in off the street covered in snow.

"Sold to the lady with ribbons in her hair for thirty-two-hundred dollars!"

Two bachelors down. Five to go.

A man approached the bar and ordered a gin and tonic. MJ mixed the drink, and then shook the empty tonic bottle at Tag. "I only have one more up here. The rest is in the office. Will you grab … "

"I will," Tanya said. Anything was better than standing around waiting for Cam's turn.

She skirted the crowd and ducked into her father's office. With the door closed, the sounds were muffled. How long could she stay in here? Surely MJ wouldn't blow through another bottle of tonic in five or ten minutes. But that wouldn't be enough time to miss the entire auction.

The reserve alcohol was in boxes against the far wall. It wasn't like she could waste a huge chunk of time in here and then claim she couldn't find the tonic. She dragged her feet. Cheering infiltrated the room. Were they down to four? At this rate, Cam would be on the block in fifteen minutes.

She glanced at the wall clock and then sat on the stool Tag used for exams. She'd give it five minutes. If it sounded like another bachelor was quickly sold, she'd take her chances and wait it out in here.

Four minutes later, the door opened and Tag walked in. "We need white wine, too." His gaze moved from her face to the stool.

She shrugged. "I was just enjoying the quiet."

"These ladies take their auctions seriously."

"Tell me about it."

He shuffled through the boxes beside her. "I thought thirty-eight hundred for a courtside Cavs game date was crazy, but then that Rick guy sold for five grand."

Rickie Seltzer the DJ? He was Bachelor No. 4, and Nick Romeo from the Cavs front office was Bachelor No. 3, which meant they were onto No. 5. *Two to go.* She stilled and listened for the cheering to signify they were one step closer to Cam. But it was quiet. Why? Was the enthusiasm waning? She hoped not. Bidders needed to keep pumped up and dig deep. If her math was right, the first four bachelors brought in 15K. That was not enough. And it made Katerina's big fat check look critical.

She swallowed. In less than ten minutes, it would all be over. Her shoulders sagged even though she knew she still had a chance no matter what happened here.

Tag held a bottle in each hand. "I'll take the tonic back to MJ too."

"Wait." She stood without purpose. What was she going to do? Volunteer to take the bottles back to MJ but detour into a back room to get blitzed? *Take action, Martin. Be the woman you know you can be.*

"Are you okay?" Tag asked.

"No." She shook her head. "I need help. I need ten grand. Actually, eleven grand, because she has ten grand and only ten grand, so more like I need ten thousand and one dollars. Enough to give me the edge."

Tag looked confused. "You want to bid on somebody?"

"Cam. I'm sort of in love with him."

He studied her for what felt like the longest time, and then smiled. "You know it wouldn't cost you anything to simply tell him that."

Like rush "backstage" and tell him she loved him? Oh, God. Her heart leapt. But there was the chance he didn't love her too? Then she'd have the pain of knowing that *and* the pain of watching Katerina outbid everyone else.

"I'd rather win the bid first, and then tell him."

He nodded. "What if I lent you the money?"

Hot flash. She fanned her face. She'd never been indebted to one person for that much money. *Don't do it,* warned her conscience.

But what other choice did she have? Tag was offering her a lifeline. His loan would buy her some time so she could have a heart-to-heart with Cam and see if maybe they could work *something* out.

"Okay." Her voice shook.

As if she wasn't already nervous enough, now she had to take her place in the crowd and fake a bidder.

• • •

"Sold to bidder number fourteen down in front!"

Cam closed his eyes and took a deep breath. One bachelor left, and then it was show time for him. His gut clenched. Nerves before a big game were understandable. But nerves before a promotional appearance? He shook his head, and hoped it would shake off the nausea.

Just go out there and smile, flex a little, bring in the bucks for Pep, and then go home. What else can you do that won't mess with the fundraiser's bottom line? For once, it wasn't about him.

"Chef JeanPaul Carter believes it's not a date unless there are candles on the table and gourmet food on the plates. The winning bidder will enjoy an unprecedented evening of culinary intimacy."

Finally a few cheers echoed through the gym. Cam's gut clenched again. He imagined there'd be all-out screaming for him. He was no stranger to cheers and jeers, but every time he tried to visualize himself stepping into that ring and absorbing their enthusiasm, he cringed. Maybe it was this silly outfit. He tightened the belt. But more than likely it was what waited for him on the other side. Katerina. Instead of Tanya. Not that he couldn't attempt to talk his way back into Tanya's life after this was over. But it wouldn't be easy. The weekend in Boston with Katerina would complicate things. And Tanya didn't do complicated. That was partially what got them into this mess in the first place.

"You're not nervous are you?"

He opened his eyes to see Jillian grinning up at him.

"Actually, I am."

"Seriously?" She wrinkled her nose. "But you love the cameras and screaming fans."

"When I'm wearing more than my underwear and a flimsy robe."

"Gotcha. So no cameras or screaming in your bedroom. That's a shame." She winked.

He liked her. She had guts. She also managed to make him smile. "No cameras, that's for sure." He wasn't opposed to the right kind of screaming, though. But Tanya wasn't a screamer. She moaned. God, he missed her.

"Katerina is a screamer, isn't she? I totally peg her for a screamer."

Wait. What? He glared at Jillian. "How would I know?"

"Oh. I thought ..." Understanding brightened her face. "I guess I was wrong. You're not *with* Katerina."

"No."

"So if you're not with Katerina, then what happened between you and Tanya?"

He shook his head. "I don't know." But he did. She got scared, and he got defensive.

"Such a shame. You were good together."

Real good. And they could be better if she would give them a serious chance outside the boundaries of this neighborhood and their friendship. A weekend in Boston would be perfect for that. He could show her his place, his friends, his life, and maybe they could figure out a way to meld their two lives into one. But under the circumstances how would he get her to agree?

The noise beyond the curtain increased when the auctioneer said, "Going once. Going twice."

He scoffed. "I can't do this."

"What? The auction? You have to do the auction. You're up next! You're the big money bachelor."

"Sold!" The crowd roared again.

Panic drained all the blood from his head, and he grabbed Jillian by the wrists. "Listen to me. Katerina Kloss is holding a ten-thousand-dollar cashier's check. If I walk out there, she'll win, and for all I know Tanya will think it was planned that way by me and Katerina. It wasn't. I want Pop to get the money he needs to save the gym, but I don't want to screw things up anymore between Tanya and me."

"She'll understand."

"Will she?"

"Simmons, you're up next," called the stagehand.

He winced.

Jillian grabbed onto him. "What if I outbid Katerina?"

He exhaled and made room for a glimmer of hope. "That would be awesome."

"Especially if we've already reached the thirty-grand goal. We have to be close. Then it won't matter that my bid doesn't have any money behind it."

So much for hope. "We're not going to do that. Pop needs to make as much money as he can." And then the solution appeared like a wide receiver in the end zone after blown coverage. He pulled her aside. "You're going to bid, and you're going to have the money behind it. My money. I'll cover the cost. Bid as high as you need to in order to win me."

"You want me to win you?"

"No, I want me to win me."

"That takes self-absorption to a whole different level."

He chuckled. "You know exactly where I'm going with this. I want me to win me so I can give me to T."

"Again, there's a little self-absorption in there, but you mean well." She punched his upper arm. "Consider it done."

And not a moment too soon for just then the auctioneer said, "Ladies, it's the moment you've all been waiting for!"

"Simmons, you're on," called a stagehand. "Now!"

God, he hoped this worked.

Chapter Seventeen

Cam stepped on stage in his silk boxer's getup, and Tanya felt the room sway. She clenched her jaw to block out some of the crowd noise. Man, if they were alone she'd unwrap him like a present. The robe clung to his shoulders and arms, and a grin graced his gorgeous face. Then, she would lick him like a super-sized, rock-hard lollipop. *Damn.* That man was fine.

He scanned the crowd, and suddenly his gaze seemed to settle on her.

Her face flushed, and he smiled. Everyone else faded away. The connection was so strong, she took a step toward him, but then the auctioneer's voice broke her trance.

"By the sound of things, our final bachelor needs no introduction. The homegrown Cam Simmons is every Clevelander's favorite Super Bowl MVP."

More screaming. He loosened the belt and dropped the robe.

Beyond fine. He was perfect. And she'd had that—all of it— but she'd given it away. She squared her shoulders and lifted her chin. *God, if you give me another chance with him, I'll never screw it up again.*

With the phone to her ear, she adjusted her grip on the numbered paddle. This was going to be the best eleven grand she'd ever spent.

"Let's start the bidding for a football-centric weekend in Boston, Massachusetts with Cam Simmons as your tour guide at one thousand dollars."

Paddles and shouts went up around her. She counted at least ten between her and the stage.

"One thousand dollars. I have one thousand dollars. Do I have fifteen hundred?"

Of course he did. Nobody was dropping out yet. She took a closer look at her competition. There were a lot of wealthy-looking, middle-aged women like MJ predicted. Except that one. Her eyes locked with Katerina, who smiled, but then her gaze shifted from Tanya's face to the paddle and the phone in Tanya's hands. The pleasant exchange turned challenge.

Bring it on, honey. Because I know your breaking point. Ten grand.

"Who's on the phone?" asked the woman beside Tanya.

She stiffened. "Uh, can't say. Confidential."

"Ooh!" The woman nodded. "So exciting."

And nerve-wracking. Tanya smiled and angled her back a bit hoping to put a barrier between her and the nosey woman. She was going to have to up her acting game. Or risk being called out as a manipulator of an auction that was benefiting her father.

"Do I have two thousand dollars?"

The crowd responded.

Tanya lifted her paddle too, and stole another look at Cam. That's why she was doing this. That man right there. He wiggled his hips and pumped his arms in a simulated touchdown dance. *Mmm*, she hummed beneath her breath. That was *her* man.

He walked the edge of the ring and reached out to touch hands with bidders. When he was in front of her, their eyes met. He saw the phone and the raised paddle too. For a split second, his brow furrowed, but then he moved on to work the crowd.

Was he angry she was bidding? But that didn't make sense. He didn't know she was bidding for her. And if he did, he'd have to be impressed. She'd taken the flashy route—for him. He'd have to give her credit for that. No, he wasn't angry. She was just paranoid. Under the circumstances, who could blame her?

She shook off the unrest and focused on the auctioneer.

"Twenty-five-hundred. I have twenty-five-hundred. Do I have three thousand dollars?"

Surely people would start dropping out now. She raised her paddle and took a good look at the crowd in front *and* in back of her. Surprise. Surprise. Jillian was raising a paddle too. Another phone bidder. For some reason, that felt like trouble. But Tanya put her game face on and refused to let it rattle her.

At five grand, people started dropping out, and she breathed a little easier. Halfway there. She wanted to holler, "Eleven grand!" and end this thing. But the bigger the scene the more curious people would be about her mystery bidder. As it was, with less and less bidders, she became more and more interesting to people around her.

"Are we still doing this?" she asked nobody on the phone.

Hell, yes. Did you see his abs? She smiled at her reasoning, and then announced a loud, "Okay!"

So this was what it felt like to be crazy.

At seven grand, even more bidders dropped out, and the auctioneer urged Cam to give a "gun show" to remind the women why he was worth so much.

Tanya didn't need the reminder. The man flexed and relaxed in *all* the right places.

"Ten grand!" shouted Katerina, shocking the crowd.

That crushed much of the opposition and put Tanya on edge. This was it. She glanced behind her to see Jillian was still in the game. They exchanged puzzled looks.

Who was on the phone with Jillian, and how much did she have at stake?

Tanya couldn't go much higher than ten grand. She had eleven grand okay'd by Tag, and she had another thousand dollars between her checking and savings accounts. Eleven-five was her max.

"We've got ten thousand dollars! Do we have ten-five?"

Here we go. Tanya held her breath and raised her hand.

"Ten-five!" the auctioneer yelled.

She didn't dare look at Katerina and give away what she knew—even though she wanted to see the woman defeated.

When the auctioneer didn't start his countdown to final bidding, she knew at least Jillian had bid too. Since she didn't look at Katerina to confirm she'd dropped out, there was always the chance the woman had more money to add to the cashier's check.

If she wanted to know, she was going to have to look. *Damn it.* Her ear ached, and a barrier of sweat formed between her hand and the phone. She looked just as Katerina parted the crowd behind her and walked away from the stage.

Well, at least that part of the plan worked. She wished she felt more satisfied. But as long as other people were bidding, her main goal was at risk.

"Do I have eleven thousand dollars?"

Tanya inhaled and looked at Cam. His mouth was open and his eyes were wide. He looked stunned. Maybe he was disappointed Katerina's bid hadn't been enough. What a sucky thought. If he wanted Katerina to win, then Tanya was about to waste a hell of a lot of money. Maybe she should stop.

"Eleven thousand dollars going once."

But their connection when he'd first stepped on stage had been so strong. He had to have felt it too. No way. She wasn't giving up. This wasn't only about interfering with Katerina's bid. It was about winning another chance at being with him. She wanted that chance. She gripped the paddle tighter and started to raise it again.

"Eleven grand!" Jillian yelled.

Shit.

People were actually moving closer and gathering around her now. She blocked them out and faked a conversation with the imaginary person on the phone. This was definitely the riskiest, most unrealistic thing she'd ever done.

"Eleven-five? Do I have eleven-five?"

Yep. He did, but that was all she had. Something had to give for her to win this thing.

She felt a hand on her back as she raised her paddle.

MJ stood beside her. "Finish it," she whispered in her ear. "You have Tag's blessing."

Blessings were good in moments like this, but blessed or not, she was still going to have to pay back the loan. How much would it take to "finish it"? She gnawed her bottom lip. Having that kind of decision-making power was overwhelming. There were grand gestures, and then there were bad decisions. She was walking a fine line, wasn't she? But one more look at Cam, and she raised her hand.

Twelve.

Twelve-five.

Thirteen.

Each increment heighted her anxiety. She needed an upper limit. She had to stop the insanity someplace. She might be willingly out on this limb, but eventually she'd have to answer to her usual sensibilities. If only the nut on the phone with Jillian would back the hell off.

But she didn't, and at fourteen grand, Tanya saw her chances dwindling. If she lost, maybe it wouldn't be a complete bust. After all, she'd have proven to herself just how far she was willing to go for him. Maybe that meant they did have what it would take to make a real relationship work.

At fourteen-five, MJ returned. "Give up," she said. "I talked to Jillian, and you're never going to outbid her bidder."

Disappointment mixed with relief. The woman on the phone with Jillian owed her father fifteen grand. They saved the gym.

Now she was going to have to figure out a less-flashy way to save her relationship with Cam.

• • •

Cam exhaled when Tanya lowered her arm and put away her phone. Straight up relief. Jillian had won. Which meant he'd won. Which meant Tanya had won too—but she didn't know it. She looked … sad. Her head hung as she moved through the crowd.

He needed to get to her. Impulse carried him off the make-shift stage. The minute his feet hit the ground, random hands pawed at his body. Dumb mistake. These women were juiced from the excitement of the auction.

"I wanted to win so bad," said the woman hanging on his right arm.

He smiled, but his eyes were scanning the crowd.

"Me too! Me too!"

"Who won? Do you know who won?"

One of them grabbed his ass. He jumped. "Ladies, excuse me. I need to change."

He fled despite their protests, but he didn't get far. More fans. More hands. He folded his own and guarded his junk. When he finally made it behind the curtains he smelled like a department store perfume counter, and he was wearing a couple scratches on his chest and God only knew how many lipstick prints on his face.

Tanya was nowhere to be found.

People started to make their way through the curtain, so he escaped to the hall. But it was only a matter of time before they infiltrated this space too. The men's locker room was the sole safe zone.

By the time he got there, the other bachelors had cleared out. Their robes and trunks were hung on a rack beside the door. He'd be glad to get rid of his getup too. This whole thing had been a lesson in what he did and didn't want. Screw the attention and adoration. He wanted those things from one woman and one woman only.

He grabbed his phone from his locker and called her.

She answered on the first ring. "Where are you?"

"The locker room."

"Oh. People are looking for you."

"Yeah, well, I was looking for someone too."

"Who?" The question came slow and quiet.

"You. We need to talk."

Silence, and then a soft, "Okay."

"How 'bout now? Nobody's back here with me."

"I'll be there soon."

He changed. Part of him wanted to leave the trunks on and use his body to sway her opinions, but lately he wasn't feeling all that showy. A temporary lapse in confidence. If she said she loved him too, he'd happily get naked with her.

The door swung open. She walked in, but stayed on her side of the room.

"Hey," he said.

She clutched the hem of her white blouse and smiled. "You were a fifteen-thousand-dollar hit. We raised a total of thirty-two-thousand dollars all efforts combined."

"That's good."

"It's great." She rubbed her neck. "Thank you."

He opened his mouth to respond, but she held up a hand.

"Let me get all of this out and then you can talk." She inhaled. "All that stuff I said to you in the car about the feelings not mattering because we were going nowhere? That was bullshit."

She was telling him.

She inhaled again, and he smiled. God, he loved everything about her.

"I was the bidder on the phone," she said. "I mean nobody was on the phone, because I was the bidder. I pretended to have a telephone bid."

Holy shit. That explained her reaction to losing.

"I wanted to outbid Katerina." She looked at the ground.

"Tanya, I'm not *with* Katerina," he said. "I haven't been *with* Katerina. I'm glad she didn't win."

She looked at him. "I sort of figured, but I worried she'd get to spend that weekend in Boston with you and things would change."

Fat chance. He would've spent that weekend wishing Katerina had been Tanya. "What if you spent the weekend in Boston with me?" he asked. "Would things change then?"

Her head tipped and her eyes narrowed. "I don't know. I'm not sure what you're saying."

"I'm saying I was the winning bidder. Jillian was bidding for me. I won because I want to be with you." If he'd had any reason to believe she'd say yes, he would've dropped to one knee. "Tanya Mary Martin, I love you."

• • •

The words hit Tanya like a cornerback with a vendetta, and her body swayed from the blow. Blindsided in the best way possible.

"I love you too." Her voice was so weak she wasn't sure she'd said it out loud.

But then he smiled liked he'd been named MVP all over again, and she knew he'd heard her.

"Then come to Boston with me," he said.

That damn realistic streak blew hot air all over her happiness. *You don't belong in Boston. That's why this will never work.*

"I can't leave my team," she said.

He walked to her and cupped her face. "For one weekend before the season officially starts you can." He brushed his lips against hers. "You name the dates. I'll make the time. I want you to see who I am when I'm there. I want to know if you can love that man. Because if you can, then we're going to find a way to make this work. Long term."

Marriage? She closed her eyes and kissed him before the naysaying could begin. When his tongue touched hers, her mind blanked. She snaked her arms around his neck and pressed her body against his, letting the heat between them evaporate her fear.

"Whoa! Excuse me." The voice pulled them apart.

Terrell. Tanya would've given him a death stare if she had any control over her noodle-like body.

"Sorry to interrupt," he said. "But people are asking for Cam."

"He's busy." Cam grinned at Tanya.

Terrell wrinkled his face. "Yeah. I saw how busy he was, but people paid good money to mingle with 'the man,' so he better get his tongue outta my sister's mouth and his ass into the gym."

That recharged her. "Speaking of asses, I'm gonna kick yours if you don't leave us alone. We'll be out in five minutes."

Cam didn't wait for the door to swing shut before he pulled her close again. "What can we do in five minutes? You should've said ten."

She smiled. "We can talk."

"You want to talk?" He backed her against a row of nearby lockers and nuzzled her neck. "Talk. I have better things to do with my mouth."

Wonderful things. Like tracing her collarbone with the tip of his tongue, sucking the tight skin between her breasts, and teasing her nipples.

She moaned.

He looked up at her with a sexy smirk. "You're not talking."

In a minute.

His brows bobbed. "But I can get you to talk." He licked the skin between her breasts until he reached the sensitive dip in her neck.

She shuddered.

"Do you want it now?" he asked.

Cheater.

"Do you want it now?" he asked again.

Always. Forever. "Maybe," she said.

He dropped to his knees and lifted her blouse, exposing her belly. His warm, wet mouth planted chill-inducing kisses over her skin while his hands held her in place. He glanced up at her again. She expected the same question, but instead, he drew his thumb in a firm stroke over her zipper.

"Imagine what we could do if I took these off," he said.

Oh, she knew!

He rubbed her until she was bucking against him, and then he said, "You want it now, don't you?"

"I do."

Sliding against her body, he stood. A kiss. A grope. His lips at her ear, sending shockwaves of pleasure through her overheated body.

"Too late," he whispered. "Five minutes are up. We'll *talk* later." He backed away from her.

She might have been pissed at his little game if he weren't flushed as hell and bearing the uncomfortable repercussions in his pants.

"You're walking funny," she said.

He made a face. "Yeah, well you're talking funny. You should up your workout routine. Then you wouldn't be so out of breath."

She laughed. And as she watched him open the door to leave, she realized life without him was too damn cold. He'd barreled into her quiet corner of the world and made it glow.

"I'll go," she said.

He stopped and looked at her. "You'll go where?"

"To Boston. Maybe we can work on my fitness level while I'm there."

His eyes darkened, and his mouth twitched. "You bet we will."

Then what? The door swung shut behind him, and bit by bit, her body cooled. Was she willing to leave her family and friends for a shot at life with him? Would she find the answer in Boston?

When she finally made it out of the locker room and into the swarm of people lingering around the gym, Jillian and MJ were waiting for her.

Jillian was bouncing on her toes. "So, how'd it go?"

The details were a little fuzzy, and she stared off into space trying to decide where to start.

"Ooh! That looks good," MJ said. "She's speechless."

"Did he tell you who won the date with him?" Jillian looked like she might burst.

Tanya nodded. "He also told me he loves me."

MJ whooped. "And of course you told him you love him too."

"Right?" Jillian asked.

Tanya nodded again. This was just so damn cool. All around her people who'd come out in support of her father's gym laughed and mingled. And in the middle of it all was her first best friend, who had turned into so much more.

She looked for him, expecting to find him working the crowd with his gorgeous smile and larger-than-life stories.

"You're going to be logging frequent flyer miles now, girl," Jillian said. "Good for you."

"He can come here to visit more often too," MJ added.

She supposed both scenarios were true. "We'll work it out," she said, and then she found him ... looking back at her. In that moment, she knew it was true.

Here. There. Anywhere. She just wanted to be with him.

He motioned for her, and she didn't hesitate even when she saw his mother beside him.

"Ma, you remember Tanya Martin, don't you?"

Clarice smiled. "Of course I do."

"Nice to see you ... " *again*, but her mouth snapped shut when his hand slid up her back in a very loving, clearly possessive way.

Clarice's friendly smile mutated into a knowing smirk, and then she nodded. "Nice to see you again, too, dear."

From behind her, someone grabbed Tanya's hand, and she turned to see her mother's shining eyes. "What a wonderful evening!" Her gaze trailed to Cam's hand still firmly pressed to the small of Tanya's back. "Clarice, Cam, I'm so glad you could be a part of it."

"There he is!" Tanya's father filled in the gap between Cam and his mother. "The man of the hour." He smacked Cam's back.

"Anything for you, Pop, but if you ask me, this was an honest-to-god team effort," Cam said, and he let loose a piercing whistle targeting Terrell. "Get over here!"

So true. She hadn't been the only defender of this gym. The auction had been Terrell's idea in the first place, and he'd stepped up in ways she never imagined. Running the gym? Balancing accounts? Ha! Her family could manage without her—if she ever decided to give them reason to.

When Terrell made it into the group, Pop gave him a hug. Her mother got in on the action too. Tears sprang to Tanya's eyes. Family togetherness. And not because she'd forced anybody to sit together.

"Hey! You really leaving tomorrow?" Terrell asked Cam.

"I was thinking about it," he said. His hand slid up her back to rest between her shoulder blades. "But with the weather and all, I think I'll stick around a few more days."

And all. She played a part in that. Tanya smiled.

"Sounds good, man," Terrell said. "It'll sound even better if you tell us it won't be another five years before we see you 'round again."

Cam laughed as he playfully gripped the back of her neck. Warm and Right. She leaned into him.

"I'll be back," he said. "Sooner rather than later."

"You'll be back for the ground breaking of the turf for sure," Clarice said.

Tanya felt Cam's body tighten, but then he slid his hand over her outer shoulder and relaxed.

"What turf?" her mother asked.

"Oh." Clarice covered her mouth and widened her eyes. "I assumed everyone knew about it."

Cam shook his head and smiled. "They do now."

Tanya filled with pride. If Cam wasn't going to blow his own horn, she would. "He's having the high school field redone. Everything brand new."

Terrell whooped.

"That's admirable, son," Pop said. "Thank you."

"No, thank you," Cam said. "Your generosity has inspired me." He glanced at his mother, who nodded. And then Tanya felt him take a breath. "Pop Martin Field should be ready in time for next football season."

Her mother gasped. Her father's eyes glistened. Her brother whooped again.

What a wonderful evening, indeed.

Tanya stayed by Cam's side the rest of the night as he greeted guests and answered questions. So many feelings tussled inside of her. Love. Pride. Gratitude. Shock and awe. This was her life, a life that on some level she'd probably always wanted, a life that she'd never willingly give up.

"You think I can play football," Cam told the crowd around him, jerking a thumb towards Tanya with a smile. "Have you seen this one?"

A few people said they had, and she tried not to squirm when Cam launched into a story about her. Too much attention, but she'd better get used to it. Loving a man like Cam meant at least part of your life was lived in the spotlight. Not her thing, but she would tolerate it for him.

"She flipped into the end zone like, *Bam! What you mean I only get six points for that?*" He wrapped an arm around her shoulders and pulled her against him. "That's my girl."

Warmth blossomed inside of her. The kind of warmth that kept you comfortable even on the grayest days. And as she wound her arm around his waist she knew she wasn't going to learn anything during a weekend in Boston that she didn't already know here.

At the end of the night, when the gym had emptied out except for the handful of people playing clean-up crew, she backed him into a corner and lifted onto her toes. This entire night had been foreplay.

"I want it now," she whispered against his ear.

His magnificent body went rigid, and she dropped to the flats of her feet just to revel in his wide-eyed smile.

"And always," she added.

He pulled her into his arms and kissed her softly.

Never let me go, she thought. *'Cause I'm never letting go of you.*

"Hey!" He grabbed her by the upper arms and held her away from him so they were face to face. "You know what this means don't you?" His brows bobbed. "The magic checkbook worked," he grinned cheekily. "And I didn't even have to get out my Lombardi trophy."

"Oh there'll be no living with you now, huh?" But she couldn't hide her smile. "I see how it is. I'm going to have to spend the rest of my life cutting that ego of yours down to a manageable size.

"Rest of your life?" His dark eyes sized her up, affection shining in his gaze. "That a deal?"

Yeah, it was. Strings and all.

About the Author

Elley Ardenis a born and bred Pennsylvanian who has lived as far west as Utah and as far north as Wisconsin. She drinks wine like it's water (a slightexaggeration), prefers a night at the ballpark to a night on the town, andbelieves almond English toffee is the key to happiness. Elley writes books with charming characters, emotional stories, and sexy romance. For a complete list of Elley's books, visit *http://www.elleyarden.com*.

More from This Author
(From *Heal My Heart* by Elley Arden)

Beer did not belong at baseball games. Not on a Sunday afternoon when there were little, jersey-wearing kids in search of foul balls, not foul mouths.

M. J. Rooney rolled her eyes in commiseration at the clearly uncomfortable kid sitting on her left while the loudmouth behind them spewed vulgarities at the first-base umpire, who was no more than forty feet away. How had the kid's dad not said anything yet? He sat on the other side of the boy, drinking his beer like the antics of the man behind them were perfectly tolerable.

They weren't.

The jerk stood for the millionth time today, bumping the back of M. J.'s head with his knee.

She growled and faced her friend and roommate, Tanya, who was seemingly as oblivious to the commotion as the kid's dad. "You know? If I wanted to deal with drunken fools, I could've picked up an extra shift at the bar—and gotten paid for it."

Tanya's face wrinkled while she chewed a mouthful of popcorn, and then she shrugged her broad shoulders. "Aw, come on. This is fun."

Not for M. J. The rude person behind her aside, she struggled with being a spectator and would much rather be out on the field, even if baseball wasn't her game. Sitting in a stadium filled with thousands of screaming fans summoned a tsunami of adrenaline, making her muscles twitch. She was pretty damn sure she could throw that ball more accurately than Cleveland's last two pitchers. After all, accuracy was the hallmark of any quarterback worth his or her weight in eye-black.

"Fans, please stand for the seventh-inning stretch," boomed a voice over the loud speaker.

M. J. stood if for no other reason than to give her muscles some action.

"Is that a Clash jersey?" The Neanderthal behind them snickered as he poked a finger into Tanya's left shoulder blade. "That's a Clash jersey." He stuck out his yellow tongue. "Girls can't play football. That's a joke."

Right before Tanya turned around, she flashed M. J. "the look"—the one that said, "Bitch, you're dead," when directed at the opposing team's cornerback, who was heading straight for M. J. outside the pocket.

"You got a problem with women playing football?" Tanya asked, getting way up in the guy's face, which wasn't hard with her six-foot-one frame.

A few people around them stared, while others obliviously swayed as they sang "Take Me Out to the Ball Game." Right about now, M. J. would've given anything to have someone take her out *of* the ball game, because if the tightening in her gut was any indication, this wasn't going to end well.

"*I* play football," Tanya spit. "You wanna make something of it?"

The guy's glossy eyes widened, and M. J. gripped Tanya's wrist in a show of peace as much as solidarity. Where M. J. would do her best to diffuse the situation with words, Tanya, the daughter of a boxing coach, preferred to use fists.

"Ooh. Is that your girlfriend?" The guy howled at his own juvenile question.

The guy next to him tried distraction with the least-effective action—he handed him another beer. Just what the jerk needed, more alcohol.

M. J. reached for Tanya's other hand and tugged on it to turn her around. The singing stopped. People around them returned to their seats, but M. J. refused to sit until Tanya sat, too. All the while, she wished her best friend and captain of the O-line didn't feel the need to represent the team *everywhere* they went. Pride was an excellent thing, but unfortunately, this wasn't the first time Tanya's apparel got them into trouble outside the Clash stadium. People just weren't that open minded when it came to women playing football.

One of these days, the Clash was going to win a championship and, along with it, some respect. Then maybe they wouldn't become targets for assholes who couldn't run a mile, let alone suit up and compete with a women's professional full-tackle football team.

Back in their seats, M. J. noticed the staccato rise and fall of Tanya's chest as she tried to calm herself down. "He's not worth it," M. J. said. "If you get into another fight, Coach will bench you." Tanya's dark eyes locked on M. J. "I need you on the field."

"Fine," Tanya snapped, nostrils flaring.

They turned their attention back to the game. M. J. focused on the pitcher, trying not to let the run-in with the guy behind them spoil her only day off this week. An inning later, the boy beside her stood to let his father pass.

"You sure you don't want to come, bud?" the man asked from his place in the aisle.

The boy shook his head and wiggled a mitt onto his left hand. "No way. Polla hits a lot of fouls."

M. J. smiled. She liked kids. One of her favorite parts of being a professional athlete was signing autographs for boys who were shocked she could actually play, and girls who suddenly realized they had every right to play, too.

Five minutes after the boy's father left, the unmistakable crack of wood meeting leather ripped through the stadium, bringing everyone on the first-base line to their feet. The ball hung in the cloud-splotched sky.

The kid reached his glove overhead, hitting M. J. in the jaw. She didn't mind, though. In fact, she'd locked onto that ball like a pass-starved wide receiver. If she had anything to do with it, *this* kid was getting *that* ball.

And he did.

The bullet hit her left shoulder before it tumbled into his glove. She winced, but shook it off. At least it wasn't her throwing arm. And the kid … he was beaming … until the jerk behind them reached for the ball, jostling the glove.

"Lemme see it!" He sprayed beer-tinged spit into the air.

Horror flashed on the child's face as the ball rolled out of his glove, hitting the seat, only to be scooped up by the drunken man.

"Finders keepers," the guy said, laughing.

"Give it back," the boy shouted. "It's mine."

People around them agreed, but the man pretended to spit-shine the ball on his T-shirt and shook his head.

Tanya growled. "Give the ball to the kid."

All M. J. could see was Tanya's fist connecting with the guy's fleshy cheek—which was warranted, but not the way M. J. wanted to start this football season—so she shoved between the confrontational pair as best she could and attempted diplomacy. "Come on. He's been waiting all game for one. He's just a kid." She held her hand palm up. "Be the bigger man."

The guy laughed. "I think your girlfriend's the bigger man."

Tanya lunged, and M. J. steeled against her. As the man wobbled in his drunken state, M. J. grabbed the ball. She had just enough time to pass it off to the child before the guy's two-hundred-fifty-plus frame careened over their seats, falling into M. J., who felt the railing scrape the back of her thighs.

"Grab my hand," Tanya yelled. But it was too late.

Bottom of the eighth, M. J. Rooney face-planted on the right field warning track.

$$\bullet\ \bullet\ \bullet$$

Dr. Tag Howard kicked his feet onto the seat of the chair across from him and admired the image on the phone being shoved under his nose by the team's orthopedic surgeon, Dr. Marcus Kent. As far as game coverage went, working with Marc was optimal, because it meant Tag gave up his complimentary seats in the stadium so Marc's wife and three kids could see the game instead. That way, Tag could stay in the clubhouse.

It wasn't that Tag didn't like watching baseball—or any other sport for that matter. He just liked fixing hurt athletes better. Besides, being near the field reminded him of not-so-pleasant things.

"She's gorgeous," he said, eyeing the platinum paint job on the Mercedes S-Class that Marc was considering buying.

"Look at this interior." Marc swiped a finger over the screen, changing the picture.

Tag held the phone closer. He could almost smell the flawless, hand-stitched leather. The image of top-of-the-line perfection warmed him somehow. Maybe it was time for him to get a new car. Maybe this one, if Marc wasn't buying it.

"What's holding you back?" Tag asked.

Marc chuckled. "The $95,000 price tag. Meredith's off to college next year, and that's a semester and a half of tuition payments."

Tag nodded even though he didn't have a clue as to what college cost these days. He'd been lucky enough to be adopted by a wealthy family who paid his tuition in full—all the way through med school. A charmed life, he'd been told. And it was, if he didn't think about what came before Edna Dean and Simon Howard opened their Shaker Heights home to an unwanted nine-year-old boy.

"So lease it," Tag said, chasing away the memory with the power of his voice and passing the phone back to Marc. As he did, the silver box lit up and vibrated.

As team physicians, their phones went off all the time, but Tag thought he recognized the name of the texter—and it was the last name on earth he expected to see.

Squeezing his eyes shut, Tag reset his brain. It couldn't be his biological brother's name flashing on Marc's phone. Tag must've been seeing things, a vision brought on by his earlier thoughts.

It's not him. Calm down.

But no amount of rational thinking could stop his throat from squeezing shut. He turned his head toward the television to hide his discomfort, and cold sweat covered his skin. He tried to swallow hard enough to break the blockage and get some air to his lungs so he could stop the panic, but he failed.

"Huh. Jordon Kemmons has a player he wants you to see," Marc said. "He asked for your number."

Bad joke, Tag thought. But it couldn't be a joke. As far as he could tell, no one outside his adoptive family knew about his biological connection to baseball's storied Kemmons brothers.

"How 'bout I tell him I'll pass his number along to you?"

Tag nodded. Somehow the motion loosed the knot in his throat, and he reminded himself that Jordon wanted to talk about a player, not rehash their abysmal childhoods that ended up with awkward Tag in a foster home while his athletic brothers, Jordon and Grey, were placed on the fast-track to professional baseball.

Marc's palm landed on Tag's back. "You have arrived, my friend. When the biggest agent in baseball comes a-callin', you're the real deal. Do you think it's Causeway? I heard he's struggling with rehab after the Tommy John surgery. If you get Causeway back on the field, every agent in baseball will be referring players to you. Damn! How'd you get so lucky?"

"I have no idea," Tag whispered.

The minute he accepted this job with the group of physicians who covered Cleveland's major athletic teams, he worried the day would come when his past collided with his present. But he wanted this, worked hard for this—the opportunity to prove to his biological father wrong. There was a place in professional baseball for a boy like Tag, just not on the field, where Tag had received the brunt of his father's emotional abuse.

Now, it was time to face the consequences of that decision.

Tag's stomach churned, but he banished the unrest with a deep inhale. He'd keep a barrier between himself and Jordon. His office manager could call Jordon's assistant and arrange for the injured player to be flown to Cleveland for a consultation. It happened all the time. Agents went outside team medical sources for second opinions. Sometimes they accompanied the player, sometimes they didn't. Under the circumstances and with a mutual history riddled with discomfort, Tag figured Jordon would want to stay as far away as he could.

"Is that a fan on the field?"

Tag snapped his head in the direction of the television suspended on the far wall. The first baseman, Johnnie Foreman, and an umpire were bent over a lump on the warning track.

Marc was already out of his seat. "This night just got a whole lot more interesting."

After Jordon's text message, it was interesting enough, as far as Tag was concerned. He had no desire to be close to the field on the heels of that, but he jogged behind Marc toward the hallway staircase that led to the dugout. No matter what the injury was, if it happened in the seats, paramedics took control, but if it happened on the field, it was the team physicians' jurisdiction. Not knowing whether the injury was orthopedic or medical meant they both had to assess the injury. Lucky him. Tag cringed.

"Probably some drunken idiot," Marc said, right before Tag took a huge breath and stepped onto the field.

Marc couldn't have been more wrong.

Just beyond first base in the dirt of the warning track, a woman stared up at Tag with watery, translucent eyes. They were the color of a Caribbean sea and, suddenly, the unrest that plagued Tag the minute he stepped onto the field waned. Whoever she was, she was gorgeous, but the blank expression on her sharply angled face bothered him.

"She just came to about a minute ago," Chris Chalmer, the team's trainer, said.

"Anything broken?" Marc asked.

If anything was, that could be Tag's cue to step back and let Mark take over. Then Tag could work his way off the field and return to the comfort of the clubhouse while Marc and Chris tended to the break.

But Tag knew it was a concussion the minute he saw her vacant stare.

He dropped to his knees.

The wind picked up around them, tossing a ribbon of caramel hair across her face where a strand stuck between her lips. She didn't move except to blink.

Hooking his finger around the loose bend of the strand at her ear, Tag tugged it free on instinct.

She smiled, and something other than discomfort at his current on-field location buzzed in his blood. He ran with it, if only to get through the exam.

"Hi, I'm Dr. Howard. What's your name?"

"Maya Jane," she answered. Her voice was soft and scratchy. "But don't call me that. I hate that name."

He nodded, holding in the smile he wanted to release. This wasn't the time or place. They had an audience—and not just the small group of players, officials, and medical staff surrounding them. Forty thousand pairs of eyes were wondering a) what happened and b) when the game would resume. The field was one big arena of judgment.

"Get the hell off the field," a fan heckled.

Those exact words were a one-way ticket back to a rundown little league field in Milwaukee, Wisconsin, where Tag had heard his biological father spout the very same thing—because there was "no place in baseball" for an uncoordinated kid like him. And apparently, there had been no room in Francis Kemmons's life for a boy like that, either.

His breathing weakened as he confronted the demons again, but as he focused on the peaceful blue of the woman's eyes, his pulse settled, too. "What's your last name?" he asked.

"Rooney."

"Then how about I call you Miss Rooney?" Tag glanced at her left hand to make sure "Mrs." wasn't more appropriate. When he didn't see a ring, he bit back another smile. This one slightly more troubling, because it was born from an undeniable attraction— something he shouldn't be thinking about during an exam.

"Fine."

"Good. Miss Rooney, how did you end up on the field?"

"It's my job to be on the field."

Tag raised his brows and looked up at Marc.

"Concussion," Marc mouthed.

Tag gave his head an almost imperceptible nod. For all he knew, Maya Jane Rooney wasn't even her name—although making up an identity would take one hell of a blow to the head.

"Do you know where we are, Miss Rooney?"

She nodded, but then she inhaled and her eyes rolled upward with a flutter and her body swayed from its sitting position.

The team trainer caught her from behind.

"Call for the cart," Tag said over his shoulder.

Laying on her back on the warning track, the woman stared up at him. "Did I get sacked?"

Sacked? Like fired? Tag shook his head. He didn't detect an accent, but maybe she was from another country where the phrase meant something different.

"You fell," he said. "We're going to get you to the hospital for some tests."

She mumbled something.

Tag leaned closer until he could feel her warm breath on his cheek and smell her spicy perfume. The normal slow jog of his heartbeat turned into a full-on sprint. "What did you say?"

"I hate hospitals," she whispered. "I hate doctors, too."

That was worth a chuckle, so he let loose.

"Then this is going to be a long night for you," he said, thankful he wasn't the emergency room doctor who'd be on the receiving end of her disoriented disdain.

She sat again, and her hand shot up to grip her neck, her pretty face crinkling.

"Does your neck hurt?"

She answered with a vacant stare.

"We're going to board her."

Ten minutes later, Miss Rooney was strapped in and hoisted onto the cart. As Tag watched her get driven away toward the exit in the left field wall, his phone buzzed. He glanced at the text from Marc. It was the contact information for Jordon along with a note:

After that circus act, I bet you're ready for some real sports medicine. Ha! Let me know what he says.

Somehow, Tag had forgotten about Jordon, and now that he was reminded and feeling uncomfortable in the middle of the baseball field, he was oddly sorry he wasn't accompanying Miss Rooney. Whether she hated doctors or not, an evening with her sounded better than an evening spent worrying about contacting his brother.

For more books by Elley Arden, check out:

The Kemmons Brothers Baseball Series

Save My Soul

Change My Mind

Heal My Heart

Take Me Out

Praise for the Kemmons Brothers series

"Nel and Gray have a lot of fun and challenging things to face . . . You will fall in love with them both . . . For a fun, sweet and very entertaining read, don't miss *Change My Mind* by Elley Arden."—Harlequin Junkie

"…Elley Arden really manages to evoke a barrage of emotions in her readers. She really has a way of creating novels that will touch you."—Texas Book Nook

"This is one of those novels that combines a multiplicity of different elements, backgrounds, and social stigmas into a single whole that will take your breath away and leave you reeling. Arden's brilliant descriptions will paint a picture you won't soon forget."—Pure Jonel

Harmony Falls Novels

Crashing the Congressman's Wedding

Battling the Best Man

Marrying the Wrong Man

Praise for the Harmony Falls series:

"The ending was my all-time favorite . . . This is definitely an AMAZING book that I recommend to all!"—Mamival's Books

"Good things come when you least expect it—at least I did with this book. I didn't expect to laugh, cry, and fall in love. But Elley Arden did those things to me, and after that short read, I think I'm coming back for more from this author."—Book Freak

Emerald Springs Legacy

Trouble Brewing

Chad's Chance

In the mood for more Crimson Romance?
Check out *Trapped in Tourist Town* by Jennifer DeCuir
at *CrimsonRomance.com*.

www.ingramcontent.com/pod-product-compliance
Lightning Source LLC
Chambersburg PA
CBHW010310100726
47905CB00011B/3281